D0589461

ALL
honourable
MEN

ALL
honourable
MEN

A.M. Braithewaite

Matador
Unit 9 Priory Business Park
Kibworth Beauchamp
Leicester LE8 0RX, UK
Tel: (+44) 116 279 2299
Fax: (+44) 116 279 2277
Email: books@troubador.co.uk
Web: www.troubador.co.uk/matador

ISBN 978 1783064 267

British Library Cataloguing in Publication Data.
A catalogue record for this book is available from the British Library.

Typeset by Troubador Publishing Ltd, Leicester, UK

Matador is an imprint of Troubador Publishing Ltd

To peace in Ireland.

'Who here is not so vile as not to love his country?'
'…For Brutus is an honourable man; so are they all Honourable men…'

Julius Caesar
William Shakepeare (d-1616)

July 1913

The road from Newquay to Brayspont runs along a narrow inlet of the Irish Sea. Parallel to the road runs a single track. The inlet runs westward along a narrow valley to meet the rushing waters of the Glenrighe river. From the inlet's southern shore gorse covered mountains rise steeply. Opposite, on the northern side, beyond the rail track and the road, lies what was in those days the McBride estate. Then, as today, this was mostly open farmland, except where it neared the outskirts of Brayspont, where it was thickly wooded.

Opposite this wooded part of the demesne stood the ruins of a Norman Keep – grey, austere and forbidding against the backdrop of the mountains.

Our story begins on a summer's evening in July – a long sultry evening of an Irish midsummer. In the light of the setting sun the shadow of the keep reached menacingly over the road and into the trees. From atop the keep anyone could have heard their voices, clear and resonant on the westerly breeze, two young men in agitated conversation, wearily pushing their bicycles home towards Brayspoiont.

"He's one fuckin' braggart. A proper bastard."

"That he is – a proper loud mouthed ballocks."

"Honest to Christ! Could he not'ive kept his big mouth shut."

1

"Where in hell or how in hell did we ever take up with the likes of him?"

The young men wore tweed caps. Their shirts were open necked and collarless – the shirt sleeves rolled back above the elbows. Their dark cotton trousers were suspended by braces.

Sean Maloney and Eamon Plunkett were both seventeen that summer. Sean was the shorter of the two, standing at five nine to Eamon's six feet. Sean was a good looking youth, with dark hair and sun washed, freckled skin. Of slim build with lean, muscular limbs, manhood would soon deepen his chest and broaden his shoulders.

Eamonn was a red-haired giant. His shoulders were broad – his arms long and powerful. His keen sharp eyes were blue – his hawkish nose was now sunburnt.

"He should've stayed quiet," said Eamonn, "I wouldn't ha minded had he done a bit more of the fighting himself. But oh no. Not our Taidg. An what a time to pick a fuckin' row – on the eve o' the bloody Twelf."

"Did you actually see any coppers?"

"No but when somebody shouts cops it's best to hightail it. You can be sure o'one thing. It'd be our skulls that 'ould get cracked an not them bloody prods."

"Too true me lad," said Eamonn, "but what's also very true is the fact that you'd better get that mouth cleaned up. The cuts inside. If the blood's washed away maybe your Ma'll never notice. C'mon, let's wash in the stream."

The friends left the bicycles in a ditch, concealed from any passerby. They walked through a field of long dry grass abloom with wild daisies and buttercups. The stream was full and

2

flowing steadily. The boys' approach startled a moorhen which scurried off over the water and disappeared into the reeds.

A cluster of weeping willows grew there – the long graceful branches gently brushed the rivers edge. Sean lowered his head and ducked under. Even in the summer's heat the water was icy cool. Sean held his breath for a few seconds. Only the strong deep movement of the water could be heard. Then he withdrew, gasping. His jaw ached. The cut stung with the antiseptic coolness of the water. Gingerly he put his fingers to his face and wondered if the swelling would show.

After washing and refreshing themselves, the friends stretched out on the grass enjoying the shade. The only sounds were of the swaying willows, the insects and the water, ever moving strong and deep. After some minutes Sean stirred.

"C'mon let's be getting on. We'll be missed soon."

"Ah take it easy Sean. After all this is our last summer of freedom isn't it? Next year it's off to university and the big bad world."

"Well I would. Y'see we're two little birdies y'see. We're leaving the nest to fend for ourselves – leaving the bosom of the home. But have you ever thought how lucky we are to be going to a university at all. Now how many of our friends have the same chance? Look at poor old Taidg for instance. Now he hasn't a hope in hell of going."

"Do us a favour – don't mention Taidg – not after today's episode."

"You mean don't speak piteously of him?"

"Precisely."

The two friends returned to their bikes and resumed their homeward trek. Just outside Brayspont they parted company.

Eamonn continued into town and Sean turned north along a side road. As Sean walked on he began to feel more reassured – his parents might not notice his jaw after all. To Sean's father brawling was an unacceptable practice. His mind again returned to the incident in Newquay – to the silly, provactive behaviour of his friend Taidg – the taunts, the coarse sectarian language and the ensuing street fight. Sean had long come to expect this kind of behaviour from his friend Taidg, yet still valued the company of this irresponsible friend.

He assumed an unhurried pace. The midsummer evenings in Ireland were long and sultry. He felt no urgency of passing time. The road's surface was hot and dusty – the tarmac was blistering in the heat. About him, leaves rustled and boughs creaked as the balmy evening breeze swayed the trees. In the hedgerows birds chattered incessantly. The most vociferous were the starlings perched like pious confraternities in the hawthorn trees, squawking rakishly. In the fields, cows stood or lay in the shade, lazily chewing cud and with studied excellence flicked their tails at the flies.

The summer's sun had first burnt Sean's skin, but as the days passed the redness turned to a honey tan on his face and forearms. His blue eyes were deepset in a fine featured face. His facial expression was honest and reflected his innate seriousness. Sean smiled seldom but when he did it was with a magnetic charm.

Much about Sean was unique. He was an only child, born in Brooklyn, New York. He had arrived in Ireland when he was three years old when his parents took up residence in the three acre holding they now occupied. The property was a bequest to Sean's father by an elderly uncle (and one time

Fenian, according to Sean's father). His parents, thanks to their American connections, were people of substance. Not lap of luxury substance but enough to allow Sean to remain at school to study for university entrance. As Eamonn had said earlier most of their friends had no such privilege – most had already left school. Few got work locally. Some went to Belfast or Dublin – most had found their way to the emigration ports and the heartrending voyages to Australia and America.

The sound of voices from around a bend in the road jolted Sean from his daydream. A sudden feeling of unease gripped him as around the bend strode two constables. Sean stifled an impulse to pull his cap further down over his face – a suspicious gesture sure to bring an unwelcome response from the law.

"Be calm, no need to feel guilty," he told himself. For all his self reassurance he quickened his pace, clutching the bike's bar tightly. The constables were big and burly men with ruddy faces and long handle—bar moustaches. They walked with long, easy strides. Both carried carbines.

"Good evening," said Sean coolly.

"Evening," came the reply.

On rounding the bend Sean mounted his bike. The road's gradient inclined in his favour. He made haste homeward.

The Maloney family home was situated on the northern side of Brayspont. Sean eventually arrived at the wrought iron gate and entered the farmyard. Making his way to the left of the house, he fetched and iron basin from an outhouse and set it under the water pump. For a few moments he strained at the creaking lever. Then he sat down on the edge of the horse trough and dangled his feet in the water.

Pensively he surveyed his surroundings – the two storied house and the outbuildings. In the nearest shed was the family's horse cab, parked before bales of last year's hay. Pieces of harness hung from the walls. Below was an array of hoes, picks, spades and various other agricultural tools. The walls were of local granite plastered and lime washed. The pitched timber roof was covered shingled felt.

The dwelling house was also of local granite, with a bangor-blue slated roof. Its door, window-frames and sills were painted green. Rambling roses grew by the side of the door, and were now reaching for the sills of the upper windows. The north gable of the house was covered in clilmbing-ivy – Virginia Creeper Sean' mother called it – green now – in the autumn it would turn a blazing scarlet. Before the house, on either side of the door, were small flower beds of blooming roses. On the ground, close to the walls was an assortment of earthen jars and blackened iron pots, blooming with nasturtiums and cascading blue lobelia. Sean's mother just loved flowers.

A sudden movement to his left made him start. The door of the house had opened and his Mother stood in the doorway.

"So you've come home have you?"

"I was only up in Newquay with the lads," Sean replied defensively.

Smoking his long stemmed pipe, Dermot Maloney had a contented look, despite his drawn, lined face (although still a young man he had suffered for years from arthritic pains). His eyes had a dreamy distant look. His manner was open and easy going. Apart from his job, teaching in Brayspont national school, Dermot's main interests were his vegetable garden and his books.

During his first few years in Ireland, Dermot lived with a constant restlessness. The move to Ireland and its arcadian pace of life had not been easy. Gone was the fast exciting world of America's greatest city – in its place, the provincial, rural life of Brayspont. In those early years the town's small port proved a constant lure for Dermot. The port and its traffic became his 'window on the world'. On fine evenings he was to be seen wistfully watching the traffic to and from the port. Coalers from Merseyside, coastal traffic from Belfast and Dublin and of course troopships.

Born and reared in Brooklyn, he had met an Irish immigrant girl, Mary Donohue, and married after a two year courtship. Soon after the wedding came news of his Irish inheritance, this small farmstead, and Mary's yearning for home became too much to resist.

Gradually, Dermot came to accept his new life. He found the Irish a warm, friendly race. The locals soon took a liking to his mild mannered yank.

"Well Yank," became a frequent greeting about Brayspont.

He even acquired a local accent (more a measure of his acceptance of his new situation than of local approval). Frequently though, the Irishness would forsake him and he reverted to his native Brooklyn Drawl.

Dermot remained silent as Sean settled to his meal. The older man stared out across the evergreen landscape, to the distant blue of the mountains. The heat haze of the day was giving way to a low lying mist rolling in from the sea.

"Sean," Dermot broke his silence. "Tea in this house is served at six. Please try and come home on time. Your mother's not a servant you know."

"Sorry Mum. Sorry Da."

"Well! Where were you then?"

"Up in Newquay with the lads."

"And doing what exactly?"

"Oh – talking. About school and about the Twelf – s'cuse me the Twelfth tomorrow."

"The goddamned Twelfth. That spectacle of bigotry and ignorance. If your in town tomorrow steer clear of trouble."

"Course Da."

"You make sure you do," Dermot thrust the stem of his pipe at his son as he spoke, angrily emphasizing his point.

"Look son just be careful, times ain't easy right now. All this civil war talk is deadly serious. So just watch your mouth. Ok?"

"Sure Da. I'll be careful."

"Now! Now! Dermot," Mary intervened, "I'm sure the lad's quite sensible. He'll stay out of trouble. I'm sure of it. Besides he has protestant friends."

A pang of guilt stabbed at Sean as images of the fight in Newquay came back to him. He lowered his head and covered his mouth. Eating was suddenly proving difficult. His jaw ached all the more.

Mary had been out in the yard. Now she bustled into the kitchen, her arms full of clothes.

"T'is great drying this fine weather. Why I only hung these out this afternoon and they're ready for the iron."

With the conservation turned to the weather (a frequent topic in Ireland given the unpredictable climate) Sean felt relieved.

That evening Sean went to work cutting the grass and

weeds behind the outhouses. He enjoyed the smell of the new cut grass and the regular movement of the scythe. The sun set in a fiery blaze. The sky darkened from the east. The mountains, cast long shadows over the valley, and soon, were themselves silhouetted in the afterglow of the sunset.

"Sean!"

He turned to find his father behind him.

"Y'know lad you might fool your Ma but you ain't fooled me. You bin fightin', ain't you. Don't bother to deny it. Your stickin out plain as day."

"Alright Da. You're right. It was Taidg the buck eejit. Couldn't resist insulting these Protestant lads and before we knew it the fists were flying. We had to run like hell before it was all over. Good job we'd left the bikes close by, I tell you we fairly cycled down that road."

Dermot's face was drawn. He pulled on his pipe. The sweet smell of the tobacco filled the night air, Sean fumbled with the scythe handle in the awkwardness of the moment.

"Alright Sean, alright. I sure don't want to be hard on you. Beside you're almost fully grown now. Virtually a man. It's just that times are not good. Definitely not. It's not just the twelth. It's this whole crisis the country's facing. Civil war. My god I can scarce believe it when I say it. But this country is on the brink."

"I'll be careful Da. I promise."

"Son you'll need to. And like I've said before watch your mouth, and from what you've said about Taidg watch your company. You'll have enough to do staying out of trouble without someone else going out of the way to look for it."

A sudden breeze – stirred about them as the lights of the

house strengthened in the growing darkness. Though the July night was still warm they decided it was time to be inside. Sean stowed the scythe and followed Dermot across the yard to the front door.

July 1913 (The Twelth)

The next morning the sun ascended into clear, blue sky. A glorious Twelth indeed. Already a stifling warmth was spreading over the countryside. The brightness robbed the landscape of its colour – for Ireland's green and pleasant land was only at its greenest when its skies were overcast and grey.

Sean had arranged to meet Eamonn Plunkett in town. He had made his way in on foot that morning. The town's square was surrounded on three sides by shops and public houses – to the south was the town dock. The main road to Newquay began at the southeast corner of the square – passing Casey's pub and the town's railway station. Opposite, at the eastern side of the square was the town's one hotel – The Crown. Victoria St, the town's main road traversed the northern side of the square. Along Victoria St. were to be found the towns orange lodge, an imposing Georgian building in red brick, and dominating the Square, the town's police barracks – grim and fortress like. In the centre of the Square was a small Georgian building – the town's "crowning glory", according to a local wit – its public convenience. Outside this was a tall gas lamp and a horse trough. It was on the edge of the trough that Eamonn found Sean – he was, yet again, dangling his feet in the water.

"Well then," said Eamonn as he approached, "all ready for the show then?"

"We're here for a laugh, and we laugh to ourselves. We can't afford a repeat of yesterday's little shindig."

Eamonn laughed as he spoke, his shoulders shaking as he did so – his shoulders always shook when he laughed. Eamonn's was a coarse featured face, with its hawkish nose, firm jaw and angular chin, reflecting an inner strength. His smile was merry though – his eyes would beam with mischief. Like Sean, Eamonn was an honest character, though less introverted. To protect his sensitive skin against the sun he wore a broad brimmed felt hat. This was his sole protective measure however – he was dressed as yesterday in a white open necked shirt, sleeves rolled to the forearms.

A series of shrill whistle blasts sounded loud and clear on the westerly breeze. The noise filled the square and rolled away over the lough. A train arriving. With it was coming the first of the festival crowds.

Soon the first of the visitors began to approach from the station. Most were family groups, lightly clad for the summer weather. Others were bandsmen in colourful military uniforms. Many wore tartan kilts. One group stood out from the rest – policemen. They marched casually, two abreast, toward the square and then turned towards the police-barracks. They wore their usual dark uniforms, buttoned to the collar, and the familiar pith helmet of the R.I.C. The most dangerous weapon any of them carried was a truncheon, which they carried suspended from their belts. Others carried carbines, an ominous sign of the times.

Toward midday increasing numbers of people began to arrive in the town square. Most arrived from the station which had been unusually busy that morning. Others arrived on foot from the surrounding countryside. A privileged few arrived by motor car. The focal point of the day's activity was Victoria St before the Orange Lodge. Bandsmen in differing livery were to be seen practicing in small groups. Some just chatted quietly or read over music scores. There were brass bands, flute bands and emphasizing the Scottish ancestry of the marchers, kilted pipe bands.

As the parade assembled, Sean and Eamonn watched the activity, bemused and detached. They were not fearful. In no way did they feel threatened, but they did feel alien – a peculiar sense of not belonging – outsiders in their own town – strangers in their own country. Before them the spectacle of the 'Twelf' unfolded.

The Orangemen had come from all over the county, to march, for three or perhaps four hours, about the streets of Brayspont. The Orangemen walked four abreast, dressed in dark navy or black suits despite the sweltering heat. Carrying an umbrella seemed yet another absurdity. Each wore an orange sash decorated with gold and purple fringes, gold stars and crosses, Jacob's ladders and Masonic symbols, draped from shoulder across the chest and back. A similar piece of regalia was the collarette (worn draped about the neck) and cuffs all colourfully adorned like the sashes. To demonstrate supposed Orange respectability many wore bowler hats. Banners were held aloft depicting scenes of past glories. The themes were Protestant virtues, Empire, God and righteousness. Some portrayed the new king, others, a long dead king valiantly fording a river on a magnificent white charger. Those carrying banners or ceremonial swords wore immaculate white gloves, giving the absurd impression of being butlers or hotel porters. All bore themselves with a severe solemnity – ashen faced, thin lipped.

Relentlessly onward they trudged, round and round Brayspont. Thoughts of blistered feet must have been banished, or if such were entertained at all they must have been dismissed with the certain knowledge that all was worth suffering for the cause.

The din was enormous. Band after band thrashed out its speciality – all with a vigorous martial beat. The air reverberated with the clashing sounds. As the tumult grew another sound was to be heard – the continuous rolling thunder of drums. Lambeg drummers. These men marched with huge drums balanced on their chests (or their beer bellies). Vigorously they pounded on the drums with long bamboo canes. There was no tune, just a fast primitive rhythm. Rivers of sweat poured down the faces of the drummers, who seemed completely oblivious to their surroundings – in a trance, indeed, in a state akin to a frenzy.

"They call them big drums slashers," shouted Eamon, "beatin' them's supposed to be an insult to the Pope."

"Fucks sake, how's that an insult?"

"Haven't a clue, but I'm sure the Pope's losing a lot of sleep over it."

Late that afternoon the tumult of the parade subsided. The crowds retired to the town's beach, or its tea parlours and pubs. Sean and Eamonn found themselves in 'The Stag' – a pub in the nearby village of Pockoreen. Pockoreen had also had its day of marching. Here, Eamonn had been able to buy some bottles of stout from the landlady's daughter. The stout was sold somewhat covertly as the two boys were not yet of legal drinking age. The stout was to be consumed off the premises – in the pub's back shed.

From the cool shade of the hay loft the boys soon heard the slurred, drunken tones of someone attempting to sing. A few lines of "The bold Fenian Men," seemed the limit of his repertoire. The singing soon gave way to a string of oaths and curses.

The disheveled figure of Ned Ghent appeared around the corner of the pub. Behind him ambled an old lame dog, a black and white border collie. With a waltzing, stumbling gait he made his way across the yard to the sunlit wall adjacent to the hayloft.

"I wonder how Ned got here," said Sean.

"Yes. I'll bet Ned's wondering that too," said Eamonn.

Ned seemed oblivious to his surroundings. His eyes were glassy and staring. His face was covered with greying stubble. About his mouth and chin, slobbers of black stout had already dried in the sunshine.

"God's a protestant! God's a protestant! God's a fuckin' protestant! Sun splitting the fuckin' trees for them bastards, an if us taigs had a day out it'd be pishin' out a the heavens".

After this outburst Ned then sat on the hot dusty ground. He stretched his legs out before him and propped his back against the wall. He pulled his cap over his face and crooked his head sideways so that his double chin rested on his collarbone.

As he dozed in the late afternoon hat the old collie nestled down beside him. Lazily it rested its chin on the worn greasy pants which hung from Ned's sagging paunch. The dog snapped silently at the persistent insects. Ned continued to doze. Behind in the pub the din grew, and the boys could now hear the drunken voices raised in song. Flutes and drums sounded intermittently, not in tune and not in earnest. Barely a few bars were played before another started. The bandsmen had spent their ardour on the march.

The boys started as a door banged open. Raised voices were now heard, slurred and rowdy. Three young men emerged into the sunlight – one a young kilted bandsman and two wearing suits and sashes. The young bandsman, a slight figure, was being supported by the other two. Corpse – like he hung suspended from his companions shoulders. A fourth man appeared from the pub – another bandsman but in a different uniform from the first. He carried a mug of ale. He was older, with white hair and a reddened face. His eyes were small and piercing.

"Throw the wee fucker down in a heap. Good enough for him," The older bandsman bawled.

The younger bandsman was lowered to the ground and was left on his hands and knees against the side wall of the pub and was now wretching. He bellowed like some stricken animal as he did so. His companions turned to face the wall and undid their trousers. As they relieved themselves of their mornings beer consumption the oaths continued.

"Fuck him. A right cunt he's made o' himself."

"Can't handle it. Don't fuckin' touch it."

"He can get himself home. I ain't nurse-maidin' him."

"Listen to the gulders of him. The wee ballocks."

"Hey look lads! Over there!"

Ned had now attracted their attention. In the hayloft an uneasy feeling gripped Sean and Eamonn. Sean put his finger to his mouth in a nervous gesture pleading for silence.

"Look at that for a sloppy piece of Fenian shit."

The bandsman advanced menacingly across the yard toward the still sleeping Ned. The old dog, aware of a sinister intention, got up and, head and tail low, scurried out of the yard.

"Drunken old bastard. Let's give him a kicking. We shouldn't let the twelfth pass wi'out giving a Fenian a kicking."

"Right enough lads."

The men walked menacing across the yard toward the sleeping Ned. The young bandsman struck first. The kick sent Ned sprawling on his side. The boys watched from the hayloft as a rain of blows descended on the old man. Ned instinctively assumed a pre-natal curl protecting his guts and groin. His hands clasped the back of his head. His ribs and buttocks were the favourite targets. Mercifully they spared his head.

"Oh jasus! Jasus! No! I'm and old man, an old man."

The assault lasted for about a minute. Ned lay on his stomach gasping, his whole body shuddering. His tormentors stood back, surveying their handiwork. Ned raised himself onto his elbows and knees, then he wretched like a terrified animal.

"That'll do him, c'mon."

"No. I don't think so."

The bandsman lurched menacingly forward, but instantly found himself restrained by the others. Grasping his arms they pulled him back.

"Enough. Enough. Back inside, c'mon."

"Too right we're not out to kill the old ballocks."

The two boys remained quiet in the hayloft. Both now felt an unspoken remorse at not having helped the old man. Neither boy was a fighter by nature. The bandsmen had been big and burly. Their mere appearance was intimidating. Eamonn broke the silence.

"Well, what could we have done? We weren't fit for the likes of them. They'd have beat the shite outta us."

"Oh for God's sake Eamonn," Sean cut in.

"We'd no fuckin' choice Sean."

"Fucks sake. We're a pair o' chickens and let's admit it. We should a done something. Gone for help at least."

The boys became silent again – full of disgust at themselves and at the scene in the yard below. The old man got up, but the shock had been too much, his legs failed him and he went down again. Eventually after picking up his cap and walking stick, and using the wall as a support he managed to stand up. With a shuffling gait, Ned left the yard, trailing his feet like a cripple.

"Well at least he seems none the worse for it."

"Oh for Christ's sake Eamonn! Enough of conscience saving. Let's get the fuck home."

August 1913

J uly passed into August. The days were still warm but the evenings were cooler and dusk came earlier with each passing day. The clear blue skies of midsummer had gone. More often the atmosphere was dull and heavy, the skies grey and rain more frequent. The landscape took on deeper hues of green due to the absence of strong sunlight. Some of the days were what the Irish would typically call 'soft' – the sky grey, with thin low cloud illumined with an all pervading brightness. The air on these 'soft' days was mild and damp. The landscape's more distant features seeming closer to the eye, yet still less distinct.

One of these soft August days found Eamonn and Sean by the banks of the Rosseena, fishing. On the opposite bank a path ran alongside the river to an arched granite bridge which carried the main Brayspont-Kilcool road. Near the two friends, on the river's west bank stood a number of stone cottages, with slated roofs – their facades covered in climbing ivy. The friends sat close to the cottages, their long fishing poles projecting over the river toward the path opposite. Here the river ran steady and deep. The surface rippled and swirled in the strength of the flow, Eamonn sat bolt upright, idly chewing a piece of grass, Sean lay on his back, his legs crossed, his hands clasped behind his head, blankly gazing skyward, The river bank was lined with trees here – ash and sycamore, their lower boughs gracefully swept the water. The full rich greenness of their foliage reflected in the deep silent water. Midge clouds hung suspended in the air as if defying the water's movement.

Two swans approached. Majestically they surveyed their domain as the glided effortlessly over the water, Eamonn gently tossed the remnants of his lunch into the water and the birds responded quickly, gracefully arching their long necks down to the water to receive the treat.

The sound of hoof beats roused the two friends. A lone rider appeared on the path further upstream, at a bend where the stream and the path emerged from a copse of beech trees. The rider was a young man of athletic build. He sat astride a chestnut gelding, The horse was handsomely marked with white 'socks' on each leg. The rider wore a black wool coat, black knee boots and brown riding breeches. Horse and rider approached at a regular pace – drumming the dry path. The horse slowed to a trot on passing the two fishermen.

"Hello Sean! Nothing better to do old chap?" the rider shouted over the river.

"Oh! Oh! Robert! Didn't realize it was you! Just waiting on the fish to bite. How's life with you?"

"Struggling on old chap. Struggling on."

With that the young man gently dug the horse's flanks and cantered on down the path.

"Well now," said Eamonn sarcastically, "struggling on is he? I'll bet life's a real struggle to him, with his fine horse and his fancy riding breeches. Didn't know you were friendly with the protestant gentry?"

"And just how did you know he was protestant gentry?"

"With his old chap this and his old chap that. English public school stuff. Now he's hardly a Fenian is he? To me that's just typical of that lot. Pathetic affectation of English mannerisms."

"Bigot."

"Who's a bloody bigot?"

"Oh give over Eamonn. He's not such a bad lad. His name's Robert McBride. I met him once or twice about town – got talking to him."

"Robert McBride! Robert McBride! Not one of the McBrides from the McBride estate?"

"Yes! Exactly!"

"Well that's a good one. That crowd don't normally acknowledge the rest of humanity never mind the local taigs. Actually they're a shower of black bastards."

"Fucks sake Eamonn. What the hell is that about? If the fella' wants to be friendly I'm not the one to snub him. What's bothering you? The fact that he's rich or the fact that he's a prod?"

"Both!"

"Eamonn you're a bigot. An honest bigot mind. Now I was dozing peacefully and I'd like to continue with that."

"Bore!" Eamonn insisted on the last word.

The friends lapsed into silence, then they became aware of another approaching horse. This time the regular rhythm of hoof beats was accompanied by the grinding of carriage wheels. From around the copse of beech trees a pony and trap emerged. The driver was a middle aged man – heavy set, with a red face, flabby chin, grey sideboards and a large handle bar moustache. He wore brown riding boots, a tweed jacket and a matching deer stalker hat.

He was very much in contrast to the slender feminine figure beside him. The young woman wore a long blue skirt with a matching coat. Beneath it she wore a white blouse tied about the neck with a thin velvet blue ribbon.

The young men's interest was now aroused, Sean's keenly so. He got to his feet and began to stare gawpishly. The trap drew closer. The young woman took off her broad brimmed bonnet and fanned her face, revealing a crop of luxurious red hair, tied up in ringlets at the back. Her neck was slender and white. Her eyes were blue and sparkled in a delicately featured face. Her pale complexion glowed with the smoothness of fine porcelain. The trap passed directly opposite. For an instant her eyes met Sean's. Almost as quickly she averted her gaze, flushing slightly as she did so. The trap rumbled on. Sean's gaze followed.

"Jesus she's beautiful. Really beautiful. Who is she Eamonn?"

"Haven't the foggiest idea. One of the other side though. Seen her coming out of the Church of Ireland a few Sundays."

"My God but she's really something."

"Forget about it. N'ere the twain Sean. N'ere the twain. You've no hope there."

Eamonn extended a comforting hand to his friend's shoulder. A restlessness now stirred within Sean. Still looking to where the trap had just disappeared he felt something ache in the pit of his stomach.

"Let's pack this in Eamonn. I guess the fish have all gone to sleep."

"Yeah. Let's go. I'm kinda pissed off myself."

September 1913

Throughout Ireland and Britain, the subject of Home Rule was probably the most frequent topic of conversation. From parliament to pub, Britain's Irish question was the most prominent, contentious and bitter of political issues. The Irish Nationalists were optimistic about Home Rule, in spite of fierce opposition from the Irish Protestants led by Edward Carson a Dublin Lawyer. The populace of Brayspont were not spared the passions of the raging controversy.

As the sun set over Brayspont, Robert McBride and Willie Adams sat on a wooden bench at the edge of Brayspont's cricket ground. This was situated behind the town's Church of Ireland – an open common surrounded by mature deciduous trees – oaks, beech, sycamores still in their summer greenery. Robert and Willie sat facing the evening sun which was now setting in a blaze of yellow, silhouetting the great trees on the west of the green. The men were dressed for the game, and their clothes were now tinged with the golden glow of the sunset. Robert sat, shoulders forward, his elbows resting on his knees – his hands clasped. Willie stretched his legs in front of him – his back reclining on the bench. He rested a cricket bat on one shoulder. Having discussed the evening's play, the conversation was now turned to the vexed question of Home Rule.

Willie dug at the earth with his heels as he spoke, "Look we can't just sit on the fence. We've just got to get involved. Our own community will demand it of us."

"Right Willie. I know you're right. But I've no real stomach for it all. All this fightin' talk is okay for the politicians. We'll be caught up in a conflict that's not of our own making or liking. But in a civil war it's so hard not to take sides. Neither of the contending factions will make allowance for fence sitters. They'll involve you whether you like it or not."

"It'll hardly affect us anyway, 'cos we're not of military age yet."

"What! Jesus Christ Willie have you lost your marbles altogether? We're both almost eighteen. That's old enough to have to shoot and get shot! They'll be murdering all and sundry! And I mean both sides. Don't kid yourself.!"

"Yeah I suppose you're right. But I don't wanna kill anyone. I just don't feel strongly enough about all this."

"Same wi'me. You know I got Catholic friends. And their alright. I mean really alright. I don't wanna fight them. I just don't see what for."

"Maybe we should just quit. Head for America. A brand new start in a big new country. Leave all this madness behind. I've an uncle in New York. Why not?"

"Well I'll tell you why not. 'Cos that's runnin'. And I ain't for runnin' no matter what. Besides – maybe this is all talk. Hot air. Bullshit. It could all blow over an be settled peacefully."

"I don't know Bob – sometimes runnin' makes a lot of sense."

"You know Willie this is one mean bastard of a conversation. Let's talk about something else. Even better idea – lets go home. It's getting late."

The two friends rose from the bench and strolled across the green toward the gate. The sky was darkening – the orange of the sunset had now turned a deep crimson. In the eastern sky the rising moon cast a steel girdle about the gathering cloud.

★ ★ ★

The first Monday of September saw Eamonn and Sean returning to school for their final year. Both were hoping to get places at Dublin's Trinity College the following year. They were keen and ambitious. Both were prepared for a year of study. They were aware of the prospects for change in their young lives. They talked much of paths to be chosen – of possible crossroads – of forks in those roads and of possible partings. All in the future of course, but a not too distant future. The forces for change were now quickening their pace.

The boys attended the Christian Brothers School in Newquay. This was an old building on the eastern outskirts of the town. A crumbling ruin in itself, it stood at the foot of an imposing hill, atop which were, according to local tradition, the ruins of the town's medieval monastery. The latter, according to the brothers, had been despoiled by that most avaricious and lecherous of monarchs, Henry Vlll. Of all England's scoundrels, Henry, heretic and debauch, was the brothers favourite – favourite target that is.

The brothers were a pious and undoubtedly selfless group. The order was founded to help Catholic education in particular. The latter was continually in a state of struggle. At one stage in the not too recent past it had been illegal for a Catholic to be educated at all. Hence the brothers were held in considerable affection by the citizens of Newquay.

The day was grey and unusually cool for September. A steady drizzling rain was falling. Sean sat stretching carelessly in his chair, staring out of the window at the rain falling on the school's sports field. The classroom was filled with a general hubbub as the students chatted idly. Their teacher, the frail and elderly Brother Dempsey was as usual late for class after lunch. The students had indulged their usual jokes about the old man's lunchtime pints of porter and had settled to an extended lunch break themselves.

Dempsey taught Religion and History. Quite a combination for the amiable but often bigoted brother. For Dempsey, The British Empire was responsible for most of the wickedness in the world. With its dissolution must surely come God's kingdom on earth. To illustrate the imminence of his apocalyptic vision Dempsey would constantly refer to current war mongering of the King, the Kaiser and the Tsar (for the catholic French, Dempsey had a soft spot).

Predictably with about five minutes of class remaining Dempsey arrived. Clean shaven cheeks glowing, eyes twinkling merrily behind his gold rimmed glasses, Dempsey rubbed his hands mischievously.

★ ★ ★

Later Eamonn and Sean were trudging home along the river bank path. In spite of the cold and the steadily drizzling rain the boys were not in any hurry. The over hanging trees were heavy with moisture. A constant dripping could be heard as water drops fell on the path. The only other sound was the rushing of the river. Sean broke the silence.

"Keegan's hopin' to go to Queen's next year. He's crazy. It's a fine university, but not for love nor money would I wanna be anywhere near Belfast next year."

"Too right," replied Eamonn. "Belfast'll be no place for fenians if this Home Rule business takes a turn for the worst. Be safer down in Dublin b'God. The protestants are threatening civil war and I reckon they mean business."

"Could all be bluff y'know."

"Don't think so – they're organising and drilling."

"Drilling – with broomsticks," said Sean.

"Broomsticks today, guns tomorrow," Eamonn waved a finger prophetically as he spoke, "besides, if they already had the guns they might not want to display 'em just yet. No need to push the government too far, Not just yet. Least that's what my auld boy says."

"And just where do you reckon they're gonna get these guns from?"

"Well – and my auld boy says this as well – they've got wealthy and powerful friends in England, Canada and in your old homeland also. Y'know them WASPS your dad was on about. Well – help from them. No problem. Not to mention the old Kaiser trying to stir things up here. Why not? He's been stirring things up just about everywhere else."

The friends lapsed into silence again. Then their attention was caught by the sound of hoof beats. A rider was approaching. Rounding a bend in the path, the rider and pony approached at a canter. The rider was distinctly female – riding side-saddle. She wore a long dark blue skirt and matching short coat. Her hat was also dark blue with a veil over the brow. She carried a short riding crop. The pony, was a handsomely marked chestnut Conemara – a breed renowned for reliability and gentility.

The boys stood in silence as the rider drew nearer. Sean was now staring fixedly. As she drew nearer still Sean noticed the crop of light red hair under the riding bonnet. This was the same young woman he had seen barely a week ago on this very pathway as he and Eamonn had been fishing. Passing, her eyes for an instant met Sean's. Quickly she averted her gaze and urged the pony onward. Sean watched as pony and rider continued down the path. She turned right at the main road. As she crossed the stone arched bridge that carried the road toward town, she turned her head to gaze up river at the figures on the river bank. The little pony reared slightly and then cantered briskly out of sight.

Eamonn had silently watched his friend's reaction to the reappearance of this beautiful stranger. He noted the interplay of gazes, and the enigma of the girl. Even her veiled face begged the question 'who was she?' The sense of mystery so compellingly added to her allure.

Sean stood still silently looking at the bridge. Eamonn placed a reassuring hand on his friend's shoulder.

"Sean. C'mon lad. Remember what I told you. N'ere the twain should meet. Remember. You'll only annoy yourself if you entertain thoughts of that un."

Sean smiled in acknowledgement of his friend's concern. Without speaking they resumed their way homeward. A sudden gust of cold wind whipped along the river bank. About them the trees swayed – leaves rustling in the chill air. Soon the leaves would fall, but for now they still sheltered the little pathway. The rain was falling heavier. The sky began to darken from the west.

★ ★ ★

That night the wind increased to a full gale. About the Maloney's small farmstead the wind howled, whistled and at times seemed even to roar. The heavy rain churned the unpaved farmyard to a quagmire of mud. From the outbuildings could be heard a constant banging – something had come free in the gale. A crack of light appeared around the doorway of the house, Then a solitary figure emerged, clad in a storm cape and Wellington boots. It was Sean. He was carrying a tilly lamp. He held it out before him to illuminate his path. The light glistened on the cape and on the puddles as Sean surveyed the scene before him. The banging persisted – demanding in its urgency. Sean quickly saw that all the doors of the outhouses were closed. He moved across the yard to discover the source of the noise. The mud squelched and slapped as he strode round the back off the barn. Suddenly the black of the night was gone. For a few moments everything about him, farmyard, fields, trees, driving rain, was illumined in vivid blue light. The darkness returned as suddenly as it left, leaving Sean with his lamp as his only light source. Then it came down like an artillery barrage – a rolling crash of thunder seeming just over his head. The flash of lightning had been enough for Sean to see the source of his problem – a shutter in the hayloft was swinging free in the wind. He made his way into the stable and ascended the loft. He secured the shutter with a piece of twine and promptly returned below.

Before returning to the house he checked the family's mare. Surprisingly the animal was not at all unsettled by the storm. At Sean's approach the mare snorted and stamped the stable floor with her front hooves. Gently Sean ran his palm down the animal's neck, patting her and talking softly into its ear. As the old horse seemed calm, Sean felt reassured and returned to the house. On reaching the front door the scene was again illumined by another vivid blue flash. This time the thunder seemed to roll deeper and closer. Sean went inside and extinguished his lantern.

"Sean!" his Mother called out, "Leave your wet things out in the hall."

"Alright Mum!" he called back.

"Well? What was it?" she enquired as he entered the kitchen.

"Ah t'was the window in the hayloft. Glass was broke in it anyway. I used a bit o' twine to fix it. That'll do for the night but I'll nail it down tomorrow. Be more permanent then."

"How's the mare?" asked his father.

"Old Betty's fine. Take more'n a bit o' thunder to scare old Betty."

"Too right son," his father chuckled, "if only some of us humans had the tolerance of that noble beast."

"Dermot Maloney!" shouted Mary, "that'll do your sarcasm."

"Sorry dear, sorry. Wasn't getting at you. Though mind you I wish you wouldn't run round blessing yourself in front of every holy picture in the house every time we've a bit of a storm."

"Godless man," muttered Mary. She was at the stove checking a bread pan. Using the ends of her apron to protect her hands she lifted the pan and, walking over to the table, tossed out a wheaten farl, steaming hot.

"Cut and butter Sean, I'll make some fresh tea."

Sean quickly sliced the hot loaf and spread thick pats of melting butter. As he did his father rose and reached for a bottle of whiskey on the mantelpiece.

"Aah just the stuff for a raw night. What d'you say Mary?" Dermot gleefully eyed the mellow golden liquor as he spoke.

"I suppose what I'd say would hardly count. You're settin' a fine example."

"God's sake, the lad's near of age now. Besides I wouldn't be at all surprised if he hasn't already sampled a few out the back of Ma Casey's. Right Sean?"

"Well not just yet Dad," Sean lied.

Mary served tea and Dermot added a small portion of whiskey to each cup. He raised his cup. As he did another blinding squall of rain lashed the kitchen windows.

"Well here's to Ireland and all who sail in her."

★ ★ ★

The storm had been unusual that September. Mostly the weather was fine. These were days of clear blue skies and warm breezes – the nights were cold and the night skies starry. Brayspont's farming community was busy with the harvest.

It was late on one of these fine September afternoons and

Willie Adams was walking home along a narrow path just outside the town. He had been fishing at the estuary of a small river. Over his left shoulder was suspended a fishing pole. From his right hand hung two sea trout – the silver backs and white bellies sparkled in the autumn sunshine.

The surrounding countryside was one of small enclosed fields on the round contours of rolling drumlins. Some of the fields were grazing a few cattle or sheep. Others were covered in the rich green leaves of what had until recently been the country's staple crop, the potato. Nearer town the last few fields held crops of golden barley. In one such field , workers were taking in the harvest. The older men strained behind the big scythes, brows sweating, shoulders bronzed from the sun. About them, boys were gathering the barley into sheaves. In the shade of a sycamore tree younger children ate sandwiches and drank cool milk from enamel mugs. In their midst sat a matronly but still young woman. Her hair was tied back from her sunburnt face by a royal blue kerchief – her white cotton blouse fitted snugly about her full breasts. Willie gazed but briefly in admiration – and wisely briefly – for he could not forget that she was married.

"Hello there," a voice called from behind him. Willie turned to see Robert McBride leading a grey sorrel. He was clad in riding boots and breeches, a white shirt open at the neck and a soft tweed cap.

"Robert. Well how are you then?"

"Oh I'm fine. Just been keeping an eye on father's fields – he wants this harvest in soon."

"These your dad's workers then? Must say you've caught me by surprise. Didn't hear you approach."

"Yes that's obvious. You were so engrossed in admiring the scenery."

Willie chuckled.

"You don't miss much yourself. Who is she anyway?" he nodded in the woman's direction.

"Dunnegan. She's Rueben's wife."

"Dunnegan. Catholics. Your old man employs catholics?"

"Now Willie me lad nothing wrong in that. They're honest decent people. This family have always worked for my dad. And his dad before him. Besides, you'll hardly mind that will you. When you think what you just had in mind for one of them."

Both laughed at the innuendo. "All them kids aren't hers I take it," continued Willie.

"No, not all of them. She's still a bit young for a squad that size. But enough of that. Where you off to? Back to town?"

"Yes. You going that way?"

Robert was going that way, and so kept his friend company for a short distance. The friends walked home along the dusty road. The sun was sinking lower in the western sky. Shadows were growing longer and the air cooler. Ripples spread over the sea of uncut barley in the fields. Robert started as two loud bangs rent the air. Gunfire.

"My God Robert you're jumpy. Just someone shooting crows. Farmers do shoot crows this time of year you know. You're farming stock yourself."

"Damn sure I'm nervous. Especially when I can't see just who's shootin' and which way he's aiming."

"Shotguns are part of country life Robert. Who shoots for your old man then? Obviously not you."

"Too sure it's not me. And these next few fields just here aren't ours."

"Well there's your gunman. Ned Williams out banging at the crows."

Willie pointed in the direction of a stockily built man standing in the nearby cornfield. Williams' shotgun was broken at the breech – the thin wisps of smoke still in evidence – the barrels suspended harmlessly downward. He held the gun in his right hand – his finger still on the trigger, the butt of the stock wedged between his elbow and lower rib. At his feet were a collection of spent cartridges.

"Afternoon," called Williams.

"Afternoon," Robert replied.

"Them crows botherin' your barley that much Mr. Williams?" called Willie.

"Indeed they are the whore's bastards," shouted Williams.

"Well now Mr. Williams I wouldn't take it so personal if I were you. I mean them crows probably don't realize its your barley they're eating."

Williams turned and glared at Willie, "I'll thank you to keep your smart arse sense of humour to yourself young fella."

"Only funnin' Mr. Williams, no harm meant," Willie shouted back.

"For Christ's sake Willie there's no sense in rowling him. Come on," Robert pulled Willie's arm as he spoke, ushering him away from trouble.

"C'mon now Robbie. He's hardly gonna shoot us for that is he?" Willie chuckled – delighted at his 'dig' at the humourless Williams.

"Let's not wait around to find out. From the look on his face right now he looks mean enough. Let's not provoke him."

Some yards further down the road the friends halted yet again. Dead crows were hanging on the barbed wire fence. From their limp wings their tattered feathers fluttered in the breeze. Their open beaks gaped skyward. Their throats were impaled on the barbs of the wire, matting their breast plumage with their blood which dripped steadily onto the road.

"Gruesome enough Willie. I guess you were right. He sure has got it in for them crows. The man's a bloody savage."

"Robert."

Willie paused, a look of bewilderment on his face.

"Robert. Oh what the hell. They're only crows."

★ ★ ★

The last Sunday of that September was bright and clear. About the church of Ireland in Brayspont, the tall lombardy poplars swayed gently in the mild westerly wind. At one minute to noon the great oaken front doors opened and members of the congregation began to descend the steps to the road. All were attired in their Sunday best – the women in long elegant dresses, frock coats and broad brimmed hats – the men with high white starched collars and tweed coats. The older men carried canes or umbrellas. Many wore bowler hats – these men carried themselves with an authorative air.

Little groups of people then gathered together to chat in the roadway. The more prosperous made their way to their family cabs and set off for home. Some family groups strolled off on foot. These latter either lived close to church or could not afford personal transport.

This then was (and in some respects still is) the usual scene outside any Irish church on Sunday morning. Church going was not merely worship, it was a social event – a chance to meet friends, to gossip, and to talk over social events. In those days the big event was of course Home Rule. So there was little of the usual laughter. The people were in somber mood.

Robert McBride stood amidst one group of younger men. A tall lean youth beside him was speaking.

"Well it's not before time. I'll be joinin' up anyway."

"Me too," said another.

"Good for the Major. Everywhere else is organized but us," said another.

"How about you Robert? You goin' as well aren't you?" The tall lean youth addressed Robert with a long searching look. His face narrow with fine features and bitter thin lips. He chewed at a thin piece of straw that was clenched in his teeth. His pale blue eyes were hard and cold. Robert averted his gaze downward.

"Yes. Yes – I expect so. I'll do my bit," Robert replied sounding not at all convincing.

"Robert! Robert! Come on! Father's waiting," Robert turned to see his sister at his side, tugging at his elbow.

"Ok. Coming!" he replied with almost exultant relief for the timely reprieve.

"See you lads."

"See you Robert. See you Andreena," the group replied in chorus. Andreena turned and smiled at the group. It was a radiant, sparkling smile that needed no words for company and Andreena did not speak. With a velvet gloved hand she adjusted her red hair beneath her hat, and then turned, took her brother's arm and walked him toward the awaiting cab.

The company gazed admiringly after Andreena as she went.

"Lovely. Absolutely lovely. Oh the good lord knew what he was doing when he created that," said one of the group.

"And a wonder what the good lord thinks of the designs you have on her?"

At that there was a chorus of guffaws and "No chance mate."

When the laughter stopped the tall lean youth spoke, "Dunno about him though."

"What do you mean Bert?"

"The straw was given a definite roll from jaw to jaw.

"I mean we can't rely on HIM, the Robert fella. Not in a fight. I'm not saying he's disloyal mind. But he's no stomach for a fight. That mightn't be the worst fault in the world. But we're farmer's boys. He's gentry. He's got more at stake. Don't seem right him sitting on the fence."

"You're judging too quickly Bertie. Being quiet don't mean he's yella."

"We'll see. We'll see."

"C'mon Robbie. You can take her home lad," Robert's father called from the cab. Then climbing up onto the driving seat he took the reins from his father. With a gentle flick of the reins over the horses' back the cab moved off, the steel rims grinding over the cobblestones.

"Well. What's all the crack with the young lads then? All about this meeting out at Major Dunedin's I expect?"

Robert remained silent in response to his Father's questions, who then proceeded to answer himself.

"Yes I expect so. Well it's the damned Liberals that's forcin' the people to it. No one likes the idea of raising an illegal army, but that's how it's got to be if we're to stop this home rule madness."

Robert could feel the tension rising within him. He flicked the reins even harder and urged the horse to a faster pace.

"Steady Robert," said Andreena.

"What's your hurry son? It's Sunday. No one should ever be in a hurry on the Lord's Day."

Henry McBride paused and thoughtfully gazed at his son. He twitched at his ponderous handlebar moustache.

"All this business not annoying you I hope? Speak up lad."

"Oh for God's sake Dad."

"Yes. Exactly. For God's sake and all our sakes. You have as much stake in this as anyone. If there's to be Home Rule people like us are finished. You think your nice Catholic friends won't have their hungry eyes on our land. That's what's always at the back of their minds. Think we've no right to it."

"Well I suppose we should forgive them that. Seeing as our ancestors took it from their ancestors."

"WHAT! Nonsense! Balderdash! The vultures. This land was nothing till our people took it on. Well it's ours now and it's staying ours."

"Alright! Alright! I'll join the bloody UVF. But I sure as hell don't have to like the idea do I?"

"Dad! Robert! Please! Oh look Dad. Robert said he'd play his part. Surely that's enough. What more can he say?"

Andreena made a timely and effective intervention. Father and son glared at each other in an instance of unspoken rage. Then each turned and faced the road ahead. A cold silence descended upon the trio. Aware of the need to check his temper, Robert drew rein to slow the horse. There was a tremor in his hands though his jaw was firm set. Inwardly Robert determined never to speak again on this subject with his Father.

Outside the town, Robert turned the pony into the small path by the stone arched bridge between the canal and the river. The wind freshened from the West. A gust sent leaves and dust flying toward the cab. Andreena turned her head away and pulled down her hat brim to shield her eyes. Her gaze then fell on a young man standing on the far side of the river. He was barely ten yards away. It was Sean Maloney. Andreena discerned the gentle wistful look on his face and at once sensed his longing for her. Then, feeling inexplicably embarrassed, she turned her head away. Suddenly she wanted Robert to hurry home.

October 1913

September passed. The autumn was cool and dry – dry, only in that there was no rain. The still calm October nights brought the first frosts. The smoke from Brayspont' chimneys climbed into the night air and mingled with the mist. This smog hung like a mystical blanket over the town. Being an Irish east coast seaport the smell was not the aromatic smell of Irish turf but the rancid stench of English coal.

In the mornings and late evenings the all pervading mist continued to hang low over the landscape. As the sun rose or set the mist became a golden mantle girding the mountains, which seemed to retreat into the obscurity of bold silhouettes before the autumn sunlight. Trees and hedgerows stood in bold relief. Leaves were now turning to their seasonal hues of rust, red and yellow. The damp air now carried a chill.

One of these autumn afternoons found Sean on the mountainside overlooking the lough. He sat in a clearing in the pine trees – his back to a stone wall. He had brought some of his school books, but found he could not bring his mind to concentrate. The books remained in his satchel. He sat quietly surveying the scene before him. This clearing was one of his favourite places. It afforded a panoramic view of the lough and the surrounding mountains. On the nearside of the lough could be seen Brayspont – its small busy port and its church spires. There were alas no factory steeples. If Ireland had missed out on the benefits of the industrial revolution – employment and improving material wealth, she had at least been spared its vices – the pollution, and the harsh industrial townscapes.

For Sean, this small clearing, always brought on a reflective mood, no matter how vigorous had been his previous ascent of the mountain paths. Sean always seemed to be at peace here. Today was an exception. Although reflective, he was not at peace. A deep restlessness had been stirring within him for some weeks now. His fascination with Andreena was growing. He knew so little about her – not her name, how old she was, nor even exactly where she lived. There was a unique aura about the girl that was drawing him to her. The fact of their different religions made her even more inaccessible to him. It was, though Sean was scarcely aware of it, this inaccessibility that increased her allure for him.

Sean suddenly became aware of a presence at the right of the clearing. Eamonn emerged from the surrounding pine trees.

"Thought I'd find you here," said Eamonn, "you're a man with a lot on his mind if I'm not mistaken. Still thinking about your woman then?"

"Yeah that's it," Sean replied softly, "perhaps I've let her get to me too much. If I could only meet her. Somehow get an introduction. I know so little about her."

"Well I'll not be so dramatic as to say you're playing with fire, but it sure in hell won't be easy. Meantime, old pal, there are other fish in the sea."

"Yeah I know. Speaking of other fish can we just change the subject?"

"Very well Sean! A refreshing change of subject indeed. To something dear to both our hearts, Me an' O'Sullivan's going to Ma Casey's tonight. You coming?"

"Well alright. But don't you think Ma'll throw us out?"

"Not a chance. We're near enough old enough, and besides we're paying. The auld bitch'll be glad of our money as much as anyone else's."

"I've only a few shillings though," said Sean.

"Good! You're in good company then. That's all me and old Sully's got. So we'll just get a wee bit drunk."

"Just half pissed an' not fully pissed."

"Right!"

Already Sean's somber mood had left him. He rose and lifted his satchel. The two young men, talking of the coming evening, now strolled down the mountainside. In the distance, in Newquay and Brayspont the light of the flickering street lamps grew stronger in the fading twilight. On the lough, a small coastal steamer was putting out to sea, its wake spreading clearly on the calm water, smoke from its stack ascending steadily into the night air. The chill of the evening began to bite, and thoughts of good food, warm firesides and pretty girls beckoned.

Casey's bar was situated on the west side of Brayspont square. Behind it, to the south was the town's port, to the west the town's railway station and the main road to Newquay. Its roof was of Bangor blue slate – its stone walls were plastered and limewashed – windows were few and small, and mostly faced south. In the porch of the bar's main entrance two coach lanterns burned every evening. Casey's had the reputation of being a lively and prosperous establishment. The pub had a back room with enclosed booths and snugs – confession boxes, as they were known to the locals. The room had a sedate but informal atmosphere, and was the provenance of Brayspont's more prosperous (or perhaps as they saw themselves 'respectable') citizens.

By contrast the main bar was bright and boisterous. When Sean and Eamonn entered from the chilly October night, the bar was busy and noisy as usual. A big fire roared in the hearth opposite the door. Oil lamps hung from the oak beams of the ceiling. The walls were of paneled oak – the floor of large shale slabs. An array of three big mirrors lined the back of the bar. The word 'Guiness' was emblazoned across the central mirror. The air was pungent with the smells of lamp oil, peat smoke and pipe tobacco. The clientele came from a varied 'cross-section' of the town's community – warmly dressed travelers with baggage at their feet – dockers and sailors from the port, their clothes and faces black with coal dust – weatherbeaten farm workers and other less fortunate members of the town's drinking community.

"Shut that fuckin' door," someone snarled with all the viciousness of a whiplash. The snarl had issued from a small fat man seated on his own near the fire. The boys recognized him. It wasFred Gant. Timidly the boys closed the outer door behind them.

A voice from the bar said, "Poor old Fred. In the horrors again."

The two friends quickly observed that Fred was indeed drunk. His clip on collar was askew, his dirty white shirt open down to his navel. His demeanour reminded Sean of a comment once passed about Fred – that he often seemed not to be seated in his chair as poured into it.

"Don't mind Fred, lads," said and elderly drinker, "he's a daesin sort. Gi ya the shirt off his back he would. But he's as wicked as a weasel when he's drunk."

"Man he is that," agreed another, "as wicked as a weasel."

"Oh wicked."

The short chorus of agreement resounded along the bar. The sympathy of the older men helped the boys recover from their initial embarrassment. They then advanced on the bar but not without some trepidation for directly facing them was the pub's formidable owner, Mary 'Ma' Casey. 'Ma' looked as though she had survived some traumatic experiences – her whole appearance was one of shock. Her still ample golden hair was swept back off her brow like a hedgehog's. Her heavy set face was masculine in all but its lack of whiskers – deeply lined and jaded. Her body was more akin to that of one of the collier hands that frequented the pub.

"Here we go," muttered Sean, "the dragon herself."

Ma placed her huge hands on the counter, and with an impassive look on her grizzled face, considered the new clients.

"Yes boys. What can I do for you?"

Ma's greeting came in its usual growl, its tone strong enough to intimidate but still containing the reassurance that at least the boy's would not be shown the door.

"Two pints of stout please Mrs. Casey," Eamonn spoke up boldly. To their relief, Ma promptly lifted two pint glasses and began the process of pulling two pints of stout. Process was indeed the word to describe the pulling of stout, for it took some three separate pulls from the pump to finish the job, which usually took a few minutes. First the pale brown stout would settle to an inky black, then another pull from the pump – more pale brown stout then as the gas settled the inky blackness would settle again. At last the finished products were place in front of the newcomers, tall black beers with creamy sandstone heads. Sean offered the necessary payment and in turn received his change. Ma retreated down the bar to finish another conservation. The boys sampled their cool draughts with all the relish of robbers of the forbidden fruit.

Ma's 'retreat' left the boys a few minutes to look over the bar. The lower shelves were stocked with ales, stout and lagers. The upper shelves held the hard liquor – the whiskeys and gins that were the more popular spirits (vodka being, in those days, some oddment that the Tsar of Russia drank). Other shelves were packed with delf and brass ornaments – horse harnesses, ship's instruments and unusual curios. There was military memorabilia – a rusting sabre, a dragoon's kepi and the pub's pride, an old flintlock musket – a veteran of unknown age.

The hubbub in the bar suddenly stopped and as suddenly resumed as Mai Casey made an appearance behind the bar. She had just emerged from the pub's lounge. Mai was Ma Casey's daughter. Her 'pride and joy' as Ma called her and the pub's very definite main attraction. Her very presence gave a new aura to the place. Eyes twinkled and voices softened. The hardness of the day went and the evening became intimate. Everything about her was neat. She was small and slim. The straight lines of her long woollen skirt emphasized her petite figure – the neatly rounded hips and narrow waist. Her breasts were not big but were still full and vigorous under her white cotton blouse. Her jet black hair was tied up in a bun revealing her graceful neck and its porcelain complexion. Her white skin glistened in the soft light of the lanterns. Her eyes were vivid blue and her mouth small and pretty.

A gust of cool night air made the boys aware of the pub door opening yet again. In the doorway was Robert McBride and his father. They were immediately followed by Taidg O'Sullivan. Taidg promptly shut the door behind him and Fred Gant remained happily and diplomatically silent. The McBrides made their way through the crowded bar towards the door to the back room. Seeing Sean at the bar Robert smiled, and Sean raised his glass and nodded his head in acknowledgment. Taidg was still at the door, searching and scanning the crowd for the familiar faces of his friends.

"Sully! Over here," called Eamonn. Taidg's impassive face broke into a smile.

"Well lads I see you've got a head start on me," said Taidg as he approached the bar.

"Not really. We're just in front of ya," said Sean.

"My round," said Eamonn, "another pint of stout please."

This time it was Mai who responded, lifting a sparkling beer glass and reaching for the stout pump. As she approached Taidg snatched his cloth cap from his head and pushed closer to the bar, elbowing his friends as he did so.

"Steady on Taidg."

"Sorry lads. Sorry," said Taidg, his eyes fixed on Mai.

"Hello Mai. And how are you this evening?"

"I'm fine, thank you Taidg. This is for you I take it," came the soft spoken reply, as Mai placed the pint glass on the bar.

"I'm getting this," Eamonn, "keep the change Mai."

"Why I will indeed Eamonn. Thank you."

Mai turned to look at Sean.

"Hello Sean."

"H-hello. M-m hello Mai," stammered Sean taken aback at this lovely creature even noticing him. Pretty girls flustered Sean. He was no ladies man. Quickly Mai turned on her heels and walked off down the bar, with all the precise grace of a swan cruising along a river bank.

"Oh jasus what a woman! What a woman!" Taidg muttered from a frustrated intent.

"For a minute there I thought you were gonna leap over the counter at he. Bit of a bull in a china shop aren't ya?"

"Bull in a field more like it."

"Sorry lads. Sorry. Y'see –" Taidg's voice dropped to a guilty whisper, "as soon as I saw her I got well – excited – you know."

"You man you got horny – can't control yourself at all."

"B'jasus Taidg me boyo, you got the quare problem there right enough."

A pneumatic bulging in Taidg's groin was now very obvious.

"Hang on till I fix meself," said Taidg, wrestling with his hands in his pockets, "lie down Fred. Lie down!"

★ ★ ★

Shortly after midnight the three friends left the pub by the back door (the one facing the coal yard) and then made their way across the square towards Victoria Street. A light freezing rain was falling. The town's gaslights reflected on the wet tarmac of the square. In the cold of the night air the trio hunched their shoulders and thrust their hands into their pockets in an animal desire to keep warm. Their coat collars were up and cloth caps were pulled low over their brows.

The night's drinking left the company light-headed and loose-tongued. Eyes twinkled and their warm breath glowed mistily on the night air.

On a street corner the friends stopped and continued their merry, idle chatter. Not for long though. They became aware of a presence further down the street. The night air took on a chill of the poignant kind. The conversation suddenly toned down. Two R.I.C. men, their wet storm capes glistening in the gaslight were standing but a few doorways away.

"Now just what the hell are those bastards gaping at," muttered Taidg, "there's no curfew in this bloody country yet is there?"

"No. We're breaking no law," said Eamonn softly, "But then neither are they. The cat can look at the King I suppose."

"Right," said Sean, "but the king can shoot the cat. There's one for you. I reckon we'd best be getting home."

The friends bade each other goodnight and made their separate ways home. Sean walked home at an easy pace, despite the cold and the drizzle. He reflected on the pleasant evening spent in the pub and on the delightful Mai. However Andreena's enigmatic image was ever before him. His mind was now awhirl with an ever changing image of women.

★ ★ ★

It was now Halloween. Sean sat on a promontory on the town's rocky beach watching the children stacking the bonfire for the night's revelry. In the quiet of the dusk the excited children dumped wooden boxes and old furniture over the town's sea wall. The air was clear and crisp. The sky was dressed in a thin grey veil of cloud. The waters of the lough were still – the grey of the sky and the dark shades of the mountain reflected in its calm glassy surface. Further down the north shore of the lough a huge flock of crows ascended into the sky from a small oak wood. Every evening at dusk these birds flew the length of the lough and alighted in another wood near the old Norman keep outside of town. The birds would fly back again at daybreak. It was a ritual as timeless as the lough itself.

Sean left his vantage point and moved back onto the stony beach. A great heron had been standing in the shallows nearby. Disturbed at Sean's approach, this silent sentinel took flight. At first the bird beat its great grey wings vigorously and majestically – then it glided through the still night air into the obscurity of the dusk.

This soft evening found Sean in a pensive mood. He had seen Andreena that day. She has been strolling along the town's promenade walking her dog – a small West Highland Terrier. At Sean's approach she picked up the little dog, crossed the road and made her way down a side street that led away from the town's seafront. Sean now knew he was being avoided. He was sure she was as keenly aware of him as he was of her. He knew his innate shyness with women had not helped – but there was that other factor, hidden subtle and powerful – religion. For many their differing creeds would've proved less of an obstacle, for Sean with his inhibitions, it was proving a yawning gulf. He was now curiously resigned to not ever meet the object of his love, and yet he was becoming ever more infatuated with her.

Sean cut a melancholy figure as he strolled along the water's edge. He cast pebbles into the water and stood to watch the spreading ripples disappear. He felt no despair only a lingering inexplicable sadness. In the fading twilight of the autumn evening Sean felt his spirit at one with the water, deep and strong.

The dusk deepened. Sean turned homeward, strolling along the town's promenade. The excited voices of the children at the bonfire grew louder as he approached. The fire was lit and a spontaneous cheer arose. The smoke and sparks billowed skyward. The flames reflecting off the water lit up the night.

The warmth of the fire and the infectious cheer of the children, like the morning sun dispersing the dawn mist, caught his mood. His melancholy was now dissipated. The fire had stirred within him an inexplicable feeling of comfort that was primeval and complex.

"Hello Sean."

Sean turned to see Mai Casey standing beside him. In the light of the fire her beauty was stunning. Her blue eyes sparkled mischievously. Her skin was glowing in the warm light of the fire. Her black hair was tied back with a headscarf, revealing the beautiful lines of her neck and throat. Now Sean felt a different warmth, the warmth of desire, and now there was no confusion.

"Hello Mai. Not working tonight then?"

"Mother does let me out now and then y'know. It's quite a fire."

The two stood talking for some time. It was a frivolous conversation and yet somehow intensely serious. Sean usually tongued tied with women at last found the words beginning to flow.

Sean escorted Mai home. The two parted in the pub's porchway and Sean, feeling self satisfied began to stroll across the square. He turned as he heard the quick fall of footsteps. A familiar figure emerged into the gaslight. It was Eamonn.

"Who's a lucky lad then?"

"You old peeping Tom. You been watching us?"

"Couldn't a missed you. You made such a lovely couple. So romantic looking by the light of the bonfire. Thought I'd stay clear though. Didn't want to spoil a good thing."

"That's big of you."

"Oh now Sean she's a lovely wee lass. But I've a feeling the other one is still on your mind. You know the – the – ah."

"Well go on say it. Protestant. It's not a dirty word is it?"

"Sorry Sean. Course not."

"You're right though. Just can't stop –"

"Listen lad. That's a donkey and carrot situation. You see something you can't have so want it all the more. And when you do get it you suddenly realise that you didn't really want it in the first place. I'm afraid she's very much the forbidden fruit."

"That's true. But the apple that you steal is always sweeter. Y'know Eamonn I just don't know what I'd do without a friend like you to reduce my love life to such clinical, trivial terms."

"Sorry Sean. But if its love you're looking for I reckon you're looking in the wrong direction. Now Mai Casey's you're woman. Your kind of woman. All the love and warmth a man could ask for."

"Ok. But don't you think I'm a bit young to be thinking in such serious terms?"

"Aren't you a bit young to be all tied up about your other one? Why you don't even know her name yet. That's all part of her hold over you of course. It all adds to her mystique. She's an intangible. If this is not an infatuation I don't know what is."

"Well I suppose you're right. But right now I'm a lost cause. Oh the lure of the forbidden fruit. I'm such a sick man."

Eamonn slapped his friend's shoulder, "Well I'm sure looking forward to your recovery."

That night the two friends went to a Halloween ceili, drank and talked of women.

★ ★ ★

December 1913

he day before Christmas Eve Sean went into Brayspont to collect groceries from Plunkett's shop. He strode quickly along Victoria Street through a freezing fog his hands plunged deep into the pockets of his great coat. It was late afternoon and the twilight was deepening. Council workers were lighting the town's gas street lamps. The streets were unusually busy with Christmas shoppers and people coming home from work. Despite the fog and the gathering darkness the streets had an unusual cheerfulness.

On arriving at Plunkett's Sean found the shop as busy and friendly as ever. It was very much a small town business – warm, friendly almost a tea parlour atmosphere. The shop was 'packed' with customers – four, excluding Eamonn. Eamonn's parents were busy, talking mostly, but somehow effecting a busy buzz about everything. The air was full of differing smells – freshly ground coffee and newly cut winter vegetables. From the ceiling were suspended huge hams – smoked and honeyed. Before the counter stood big wooden chests of tea, to be bagged and weighed to order. At one end of the counter were stacked cheeses – prized gorgonzolas and plain cheddars. At the counter's other end were the turkeys, freshly plucked, their skins blue and their long, lifeless necks dangling limply from the counter top.

"You'll find your mother's things over there Sean," called Eamonn's mother, "by the tea chest. Your name's on the box."

"Thanks, Mrs. Plunkett."

"Happy Christmas Sean."

"And to you Mrs. Plunkett."

Sean took his package and set out for home. He had not gone very far down Victoria Street when he noticed a car (in those days a car definitely got noticed) parked by the sidewalk. Its engine was running. The smell of the exhaust filled the night air. A young elegantly dressed woman sat in the passenger seat. She wore a pale blue coat with an ermine collar, with an ermine muff and hat to match. Sean recognized the bright blue eyes and red hair. It was Andreena.

"Merry Christmas Sean," said a voice from behind.

Sean turned to see Robert McBride, warmly clad in a woollen great coat, hunting hat and goggles.

"Merry Christmas Robert," replied Sean.

"What do you think of her then?"

"What? Who? Think of her?" stammered Sean.

"The car man! The car! What do you think of our new car?"

"Oh! Oh the car. Why she's absolutely beautiful," said Sean, his gaze firmly fixed on the passenger.

"Aye she's a classy chassis alright. Listen Sean. There's a party on in our house on St. Stephen's night. Why don't you come along. Bring Eamonn. Your friend Sullivan is coming."

"Very nice of you Robert. Why of course we'll come."

"Look forward to seeing you then."

Robert mounted the driver's seat and moved off, the car reverberating and rattling as he turned out into the town's wide main street.

As the McBride's moved off Sean found himself gazing at Andreena yet again. This time their eyes met and held each other. Andreena smiled gently, demurely nodding her head in acknowledgement. Sean felt the thrill of enrapture in his whole being and yet still his heart seemed to ache unbearably. Then the car slowly moved off along the street. Sean could not have been happier after this chance encounter. The prospect of another encounter on St. Stephen's night only enthralled him more.

December 1913 – McBride's

he McBride family home was a substantial country dwelling built in the mid nineteenth century in the Tudor style. The house may not have been referred to as a mansion or as being stately, but it was an elegant and comfortable family home. The house contained six bedrooms, a large kitchen, a dining room and a handsome drawing room. There was also a well stocked library which old McBride referred to as the 'study'.

Not stately but definitely comfortable, the McBride home was not marked (for the rest of Brayspont that is) by its size nor décor so much as its staff. The McBrides employed a cook, two maids and a groundsman, besides its regular hiring of field hands. The McBrides were definitely seen as people of substance. Certainly to those who did not enjoy similar wealth the McBride prosperity seemed both a matter of envy and mystery.

In the main entrance hall, the oaken staircase situated opposite the front door, ascended to an open landing from which separate hallways led to the bedrooms. On this St. Stephen's night these balustrades were adorned with garlands of holly, ivy and mistletoe (the latter was a surprise as old McBride was very 'straight laced'). Holly wreaths hung on the oak panelled wall. A gaily decorated Christmas tree stood near the front door. At the left of the staircase was a big open fire place ablaze with logs and coal. A cheerful Henry McBride stood in the hallway (the 'arse' of his trousers smouldering as he stood almost on top of the fire) greeting his guests. At his side his wife served glasses of punch from a steaming bowl.

The hallway that evening had a cheerful atmosphere, with different groups of people talking and laughing. The warmth of the log fire and Mrs. McBride's punch being the major contributors to the merriment.

Sean Maloney and Eamonn Plunkett arrived shortly after nine o'clock. The first person to greet them was Mary O'Dowd the McBride's domestic servant. Mary relieved them of their coats and hats which she promptly hung in the cloakroom. The two friends stood awkwardly looking around. Their embarrassment did not last long. Robert McBride approached.

"Sean! Eamonn! Nice of you to come. You'll get some punch over by the fire. C'mon."

The newcomers were led over to the fireplace and the hot punch. A brief introduction to Robert's parents and the trio moved to a corner of the hall.

"This punch is quare stuff Robbie," said Eamonn, gingerly sipping from the big round glass, "the very stuff for a raw night like th'yon."

"Too right," said Sean, "what's the main ingredient? Malt? Scotch? Cognac?"

"Mum's recipe," said Robbie, "Red wine, brandy and spices and God only knows what else. Should be a nice evening ahead. Dances – jigs and waltzes. Local musicians. I'm sure you'll know a few of them. Yes it should be quite alright. By the way you're friend Sully's here."

"Speak of the devil," said Sean.

"And he will appear," laughed Taidg O'Sullivan.

"What've you been up to then?" said Sean.

"Well lads a've just been samplin' this wondervul stuff 'ere. A very merry Christmas to y'all." A distinctive slur was now evident in Taidg's speech.

"Ah yes of course the punch. We've just been sampling its virtues ourselves," said Eamonn.

"Excuse me a moment." Robert left the company and moved to the front door, where another guest had arrived.

"Just what have you been at Sully?" whispered Sean, this is no place to start muckin' about."

"Now, now lads. I won't let the side down. Besides – it is a party. I'm just getting' a wee bit lit up thass all. Honest."

"Some more punch gentlemen?"

Mary O'dowd' soft voice interrupted. Mary stood arm outstretched offering yet more of the potent concoction.

"Not just now Mary. And Taidg's had enough too," said Sean, restraining Taidg's outstretched hand.

"Later Mary. Later," Taidg slurred, as he winked mischievously at the girl. Eamonn and Sean detected a distinct lecherous intonation to Taidg's 'later Mary'.

Even in the mundane, monochrome black and white of her servants' domestic uniform, Mary looked exceptionally beautiful. She was small and slim with a narrow waist and small round breasts. Her auburn hair was tied in a bun behind her white matron's cap. Everything about her was so petite – her lips, the lower one making a pretty pout – her nose small and sharp. Her round cheeks were small and they dimpled when she smiled – they dimpled now when she smiled quietly at Taidg and demurely walked off to another group of guests.

"Oh Man! What wouldn't I give to have a go at that," said Taidg, watching Mary move across the room.

"You wouldn't have a chance Taidg. Not a chance. Not in your condition."

"What! What the fuck! Now just what are you getting at Maloney? What d'ya think yer on? M'fuckin' condition indeed!"

"Now y'know the old sayin' Taidg. A mean y'know – too much to sup and ya canna get it up. No offence auld hand."

"Right! Right! A see what ya mean," Taidg reached out his glass and set it on a nearby table, "Right we'll see. Come the end of the evenin's proceedin's an we'll see what old Sully's fit for. And just who he's fit for. Drunkard's droop indeed."

Just then the tumult in the hallway ceased as Henry McBride called for the attention of his guests, (I should stress that the tumult was a relatively minor one – slurred and altogether very low key).

"Ladies and Zgentlemen. Friends and neighbourz," (like Taidg old McBride was feeling the effect of the punch). "Before the dancin' and merriment begins I'd like to say a few words of welcome to you all. The occazzion of the fwestivities is of course Christmas – the birthday of our lord and zaviour. We all love the Christmas message, Peace on earth and goodwill to men, Oh, eh women too of course. Alas! A few days into the new year and we've forgotten it all. Or at least there seems to be a dearth of it. But I want tonight to be a particularly happy evening – one to remember. For me this Christmas is special. This could be the last – the last –."

Henry's wife came forward to assist him. The old man was now struggling, his eyes assuming a distant even a shocked look. Then he stirred from his trance – "Yes. Yes. For all of us perhaps. Yes. This could be the end. Too much water under the bridge now. Here and in Europe. God only knows what awaits us."

Henry McBride now paused. His face had again taken on a blank, wistful look. His watery eyes were round and staring. Then suddenly he smiled and continued, "And so my friends to Christmas."

"Holy fuck," muttered Taidg, "a thought we were in for a bit of Shakespeare, the old friends, romans and countryman bit. Well here's to a merry fuckin' Christmas then."

Midnight, and the music stopped. The company dissolved yet again into small groups of chatting friends. Already some of the guests had begun to leave. Sean's hope of meeting Andreena had been realized. At first the pair had fought shy of each other, each remaining in the company of a friend. But increasingly their eyes met across the room. The warm homely surroundings somehow entrapped them, ensuring a growing intimacy in that mutual fixation. Sean eventually plucked up enough courage to ask Andreena to dance – the waltzes afforded an excellent opportunity for conversation. Sean felt a thrill surge within him as Andreena spoke of her hopes for a nursing career in Dublin. The fact of their lives following a common path suited Sean's wishful thinking. Destiny if there was such a thing suited his infatuation, and Sean was now indeed thoroughly infatuated. When Andreena was asked to dance by other young hopefuls Sean looked on resentfully.

"Jealousy 'll get you nowhere," Eamonn jibed. The advice went unheeded if not unheard.

"Well not to worry. See. She still has eyes only for you."

For all his jealously, though, Sean was feeling very happy when the party ended. Andreena indeed kept flashing a winning smile in his direction, and he now felt securely introduced to her. He and Eamonn stood in the hallway preparing to take their leave when they missed Taidg.

"O'Sullivan! Now where the fuck is he?" said Sean.

"I dare say," whispered Eamonn, "that if we could find Mary O'dowd we might also find old Sully. I notice another servant giving out the coats from the cloakroom."

"Oh the horny bastard."

"What'll we do? We'd better find him before the McBrides do."

"Too right," said Sean, "there'll be fuckin' blue murder then. I'll go upstairs and check out the servants quarters. I'll make the excuse that I was lookin' for the toilet if I'm stopped."

Sean moved quickly up the stairs and made his way down the left landing. From one of the rooms he heard the sound of talking and giggling. He tried the door – open. He entered a small sparsely furnished room lit by a small oil lamp. Opposite the door was a bed on top off which was Mary and Taidg.

Taidg suddenly sat bolt upright and reached for his shirt buttons. Mary, a look of alarm on her face, fumbled for the buttons of her blouse.

"Pardon the intrusion," said Sean.

"Certainly not," snapped an indignant Mary straightening the tresses of her skirt, "you've no manners Sean Maloney, walking into a lady's room unannounced, without so much as a knock on the door!"

"Oh. A lady's room indeed," though softly spoken Sean's sarcasm was razor shape. "Why of course. I'll have to remember me manners in future."

"Well what is it? What d'you want." Taidg grumbled as though he were master of the house.

"It's time to go home. We'll be waiting in the porch. An' for God's sake get a move on. There'll be one unholy rumpus if this is found out. Abusing hospitality like this."

At Sean's last remark, May stiffened in imperious and self righteous anger. So angry as to be speechless. She glared furiously at an unrepentant and smiling Sean. Her pretty face, flushed with rage (and no doubt, her romp with Taidg) was never so beautiful. Sean left the room, gently closing the door behind him. He hurried along the landing and descended the stairs to the front hallway. Eamonn turned to meet him.

"Well did y'find him?"

"I did."

"Was he…"

"He was."

The friends had just donned their greatcoats when a familiar voice hailed them from outside – Taidg. The friends exchanged looks of surprise.

"How'd he get passed us?"

"He didn't," said Sean. "I reckon he was too fly for that. Probably slipped out a side door. He has someone to show him out of course."

Outside Taidg informed them that he had indeed left the house in this stealthy manner.

"Couldn't let auld McBride catch me at that now could I?" Taidg's breath was steamy on the frosty night air.

"Tis well for the pair of ye," said Eamonn, clutching his collar tightly, "amorous adventurers the two of ye."

"What!" Taidg squealed in delight. "You too Sean. Why you're the quare lad. So you got off your mark then?"

"Well not exactly," said Sean beaming with pride and affected modesty.

"No indeed," said Eamonn, "not exactly. You see, his affair is one of the heart. One of the spirit. His wouldn't be as daring as yours. Nor as dashing – nor as downright bloody dangerous."

"What! What the bloody hell d'you mean?"

"Well suppose we mean, we hope ye won't put the wee lassie in the family way. You've time enough havin' a spud in the oven."

"For Christ's sake," shouted Taidg. "I know what I'm doing."

Then as quickly as it had happened Taidg's sudden flash of anger passed and the real Taidg surfaced again, the mischievous, irresponsible Taidg was back. The daring eyes twinkled merrily.

"Alright lads. Alright. You're concern is appreciated, believe me. But don't worry I'm not for getting caught out nor makin' a fool of anyone. But what about you Sean. What about this superior, more elevated, more platonic affair of the heart of yours? We'll refer to yours as an affair of the heart. To mine, to my baser more lower level affair, as an affair of God knows what part of me. Well then? What about her?"

"Andreena," said Eamonn, "he's captured her heart an' soul, and the rest of her'll follow later. Of that we're sure."

Sean smiled but said nothing.

"B'jasus y'have. Well that's a good'n," said Taidg, "a pretty piece, a pretty piece. Clever an'all. But th'other side of the house. You'll have your work cut out for you there me boyo."

"I tell you he's already clicked, he's already won her eye. Got it?" said Eamonn.

Sean still said nothing but remained detached from the conversation, a curious eavesdropper into this discussion of his own fate.

"So what? Romeo and Juliet but it was hardly a happy ever after fairy story, was it?"

The night was clear – the stars shone and an almost full moon cast a brilliant glow over the landscape. The only cloud hung low over the mountain tops in a silver blue shroud. A frost had covered the fields and the moonlight reflected on the grass throwing the trees and hedgerows into dark blue profiles. The friends continued homeward, Sean pensive and self-satisfied, Taidg and Eamonn in idle tireless conversation.

January 1914

he night was black and freezing cold. A driving shower of sleet was falling. The wind gusted along Brayspont's Post Office Street, whistling incessantly, rising to a furious howling and receding. The rain water ran down the street in muddy rivulets, eddying into puddles on the open roadway. In an alley way, at the rear of the old Town Hotel three men stood in the shadows. The alley afforded a respite from the biting cold of the northerly gale. Robert McBride was one of the men. His companions were men of his own age – Wesley Smith and Alan Connor, both were sporting shotguns. Robert shivered despite his great coat. His feet were wet and half frozen. In his pocket his hand number as it clutched the cold metal of a Webley pistol. A tingling chill ran through him as he fumbled for the safety catch – it was on. It had been on all night, each time he had nervously, indeed neurotically checked it. Robert was terrified of guns.

Wesley and Alan, to give themselves a more military bearing had wrapped their ankles and shins in puttees, and wore bandoleros across their chests. Earlier Robert observed (with some relief) that the bandoleros were empty – the cartridges, he had assumed, had been removed to keep them dry. Perhaps like most of the newly formed volunteer force they just did not have the ammunition. But the force was no 'paper tiger'. The protestant was determined to the point of fanaticism. And their very purpose this stormy night was to acquire an arsenal.

The men were already tense from their seriousness of purpose – the cold and the wet added to their discomfort. Robert looked at his stopwatch exactly two o'clock. There was no conversation between the three, each man was alone with his thoughts.

An eerie howling filled the air as another gust of wind blasted along the street. A sudden crash startled the men.

"More slates down," said Wesley.

"Not surprising. That'd lift the best roof in Ireland."

"Quiet!" Robert rasped in an excited whisper, "Someone's coming."

Robert moved to the end of the alleyway so as to get a more commanding view of the street. His companions followed. Still standing in the protection of the shadows, Robert nervously clutched the webley. Across the road, from another side street, a figure in a billowing storm cape emerged. At first a silhouette against the lamplight, the man's features became clearer as he approached. Captain Peter Philips – lately of the British Army, now an officer in the newly formed U.V.F.

"McBride!" called Philips.

"Captain!" replied Robert.

"Very well. You know what to do. We should've no trouble. The rest of the port's in our hands. There should be no interference. So this is only a precaution. Off you go and good luck."

"Jasus a thought the auld ballocks was gonna say we kin all go home now. Fuck him anyway." shouted Connor.

"Quiet for Christ's sake. He'll hear ye."

"Above this wind. He'll be a good'n."

The three men moved out of Post Office Street and into the main square turning left into Dock Street. At the end of Dock Street lay their objective – the town's east quay and built on this, the old customs house.

Once on the quay the party was exposed to the full rage of the storm. With an intolerable fury the wind lashed huge waves against the sea wall, showering the men with the freezing spray. The men struggled to keep their feet as the storm blew even stronger. The bitter cold gnawed at their faces and hands.

Beside them, to their right, in the old town dock, small boats lay partially submerged in the shallows. The lights from the opposite quay flickered and danced on the agitated waters. To their left and seaward, all was darkness.

Suddenly the black, storm clouds parted and the moon was out. Its brilliant, silver blue sheen bathed the mountains and the raging sea.

"There she is!"

Alan's cry was swept away on the howling wind. And there indeed she was – a small trawler struggling resolutely through the mountainous sea, huge columns of spray lashing her decks and bridge. On she came, plunging so low as to almost disappear, then rearing like a mighty warhorse, defiant, the sea racing from her scuppers.

On gaining the shelter of the customs house porch Wesley tried to force the door. It was locked. Swearing, fumbling, striking, Wesley, rainwater streaming from his cap to his face, tried in vain. Robert drew his Webley. Using the butt he smashed the side window. Reaching in round the big oaken door he drew the latch. It yielded.

In the hallway the storm lanterns were hastily lit. The mantles glowed with a steady hissing and a familiar pungent smell.

The men were wet, cold and nervous. In the dim lamp light Robert could see the consternation on the faces of his friends. He knew his own feelings only too well. A fear, an unreasoning paranoia had overtaken him – Robert had never broken the law till now. He feigned confidence.

"Ok. Check upstairs. I'll do the back rooms."

After some minutes the friends re-assembled on the main ground floor office. The building was indeed empty. The light of the lantern now burned brightly. The three now felt more secure. Outside, the howling of the wind rose to a crescendo. The driving sleet covered the windows on the seaward side of the house. But the porch windows gave a commanding view of a stove – a freestanding one with a stone flue. A fire was kindled.

"Bloody freezin' here."

"How about tea? His Majesty's Customs and Excise can make a contribution to the cause. Now where would they keep the goodies?"

"Wes. Raid the food cupboards at the back."

"How long'll it take?"

"Just that long. As long as it takes."

"C'mon man. How fuckin' long is that?"

"About two hours. Not much more. Them rough seas should be no problem once she's in the old Town dock. They've at least a hundred motor cars lined up to take the stuff away."

Greatcoats and hats were hung up to drip dry. Great pools of water began to grow on the stone floor.

"Tea. Fuck your tea. This is no Boston tea party. I got some of his Britannic Majesty's contraband here. An' we ain't dumpin' this in no fuckin' harbour."

"What's he on about?"

Wes burst triumphantly into the hallway brandishing two bottles of scotch. Whiskey glasses were then acquired.

"A lock o wee drams – eh! A lock o wee drams to thaw us out."

★ ★ ★

The news that the Ulster Protestants had successfully landed and distributed weapons set all Ireland on a war footing. The rifles were few in number and the ammunition for use with the same rifles was hopelessly inadequate – so hopelessly inadequate in fact that any protestant rebellion would scarcely have lasted a few desperate hours against the might of the British Army. Such rational thoughts were irrelevant in the passion that now consumed the country. The fear of civil war was now real enough. After Robert McBride and his companions had staged their daring coup at Brayspont Port, many Irish Catholics now considered a similar course of action. The Maloney's were no exception.

In the parlour Dermot and Sean sat before the fire. The air was filled with the wisp of turf smoke mingling with the aroma of pipe tobacco. Outside dusk was falling. The afterglow of the sunset cast its fading warmth over the February snow. Sean was igniting an oil lamp. Dermot sat with a pensive look, drawing steadily from his pipe, his teeth clenching the stem in determination. Sean was in a garrulous mood.

"Dad if they've got guns we should've guns. It's as simple as that. If not they'll impose their settlement on us. The British'll not stand up to them, least I wouldn't trust them. Would you? What solution would that be? Whose gonna call that freedom?"

"Talk comes easy son. And I hope you're not thinking of leading any charges. Sitting here by the apparent security of our own fireside. And it's only an apparent security mind. We're so far removed from the reality of war. How'd you like to be out in the Balkans, or to have been in South Africa or Cuba? Oh it's a different matter when the lead's actually flying. I'm telling you. You know it always seems to have been like this. At the start everyone's fiery and bloodthirsty. Then after half the world's been slaughtered, people start to wonder how they got into the situation in the first place. War! Collective insanity!"

"I'm not sayin' war's fun. But what of justice? And we need justice in this country."

"Justice! Justice!" Dermot, now clearly irritated by his son, fidgeted awkwardly in his chair, "that's like freedom! Another much misused word. Your grandfather fought at Gettysburg son. I don't aim to forget the stories he told me. That was about white killing white to set black free."

"And why not?"

"Sure why not? But don't lose sight of how barbaric it all is however worthy the cause. Causes breed fanaticism. This here'll be worse than any race war."

Dermot now rose from his chair. The irritation was suddenly gone. Sean sensed a sadness come over his father.

"That'll be enough for now son. Mother'll be in soon. She doesn't go much for all this political talk. We'll talk again."

Dermot moved toward the back door and gazed out the window. The mountains were now deepening in shadow. In the near fields the warm glow of the sunset reflected on the snow, and in the distance where the fields seemed to meet the mountains, tinged the purple azure of the fog bank with a rim of gold. In the deepening shades of the dusk, hedgerows and trees became ink black silhouettes, their gaunt hungry forms desolating the landscape.

Sean looked at his father as he stood gazing at the wintry desolation outside. Sean was filled with wonder and admiration for this man who, for a woman's love had left the bustling life of New York to come to Ireland, remote and impoverished, arcadian and innocent.

The silence was broken by the sound of the latch drawing on the front door. Mary Maloney entered the hallway, bringing with her a breath of the crisp, cold outside air. The cold had brought a pink glow to Mary's complexion. Her blue eyes were clear and sparkling.

"I wouldn't want to be going far that evening. My toes are near frozen off. You two are looking down in the mouth. What's wrong?"

"Nothing at all. Maybe this weather's getting' us down," Sean replied with a distinct lack of conviction.

"Surely. Or maybe you've been talking civil war again. Oh honest to God is there no getting away from it? Down the street, in the shops. Now it's in me own home."

Mary took off her coat and hung it in the hallway. She

returned, gliding into the room with a serene swan like movement. Her eyes were fixed on Dermot.

"You know Dermot, I often wonder if I did right. I mean I often feel so guilty, persuading you to settle in this-" Mary sighed, "unhappy land."

"Why now love that's ridiculous. Life has its trials no matter where you are."

Mary shook her head wearily as she moved towards the stove. She then proceeded to change the topic of conversation.

"I've potatoes in the oven. Should be nicely baked by now. I've some fresh cod. How'd you like you're cod?"

"Floured and fried in suet."

"Agreed." And to wash it down I've some bottles of the black stuff."

The atmosphere changed. Talk of the good life now filled each one's mind. But fear persists – however mute.

That night Sean went into Brayspont to meet Eamonn. The two met in Post Office Street. They trudged across the square to Casey's, the hard packed snow crunching under their feet. Under their great coats they hunched their shoulders against the cold.

"Well then," said Sean, "what's this fella like anyhow? Dublin man isn't he?"

"Yes he's a Dubliner alright. I don't know if you'll like him or not. He has I.R.B. contacts. He's definitely patriotic. But he's an odd fish. I'll not say too much. Be unfair to prejudge any man. You can make you're known mind up."

"What's his name?"

"Flanaghan. Myles Flanaghan."

As Eamonn and Sean reached Casey's porch another light flurry of snow began to fall. The floor of the porchway was now covered in a muddy slush. The friends kicked and stamped their feet to shake the snow from their boots. Opening the door they felt the familiar warmth of the pub.

"You order Eamonn. I want to thaw out y the fire."

Sean moved over to the turf fire and stood before it, his arms behind his back, facing the bar.

"Hey son! Don't block the heat." A familiar rasping voice sounded from across the room. Two elderly men sat near the door. Sean recognised one of them as Ned Ghent.

"Sorry Mr. Gant," Sean replied, "just give us a minute to warm up. It's a raw night."

Eamonn joined him with two mugs of porter.

"Slainte."

"Slainte."

"Right young Maloney. Your fuckin' arse must be well cooked b'now."

A chorus of reproach now followed.

"Get to fuck…"

"C'mon out of it."

"Fucksake move."

"Fucksake."

Wisely the two friends moved away from the coveted warmth of the fire to a table.

"Well I suppose this'll have to do," said Eamonn.

"Near enough," replied Sean, "but now, What about this revolution of yours?"

"What indeed? If our man turns up tonight he'll no doubt introduce us to the right people. Joining the Irish Volunteers is one ting but I think the Republican Brotherhood would be more effective."

"Now why do you say so? I reckon the Volunteers should be an adequate counter force to the UVF. If they are organised and armed then shouldn't we? We need a similar force."

"It's not without its value. But I can't help being sceptical. If every joe soap in the country joins how strong will it be? Joe soaps aren't renowned for their staying power and when the going gets rough I mean."

"Too much riff-raff eh? You're a snob Eamonn."

"Realism I reckon. Mass movements haven't got us too far in the past. Too easily divided and bought off by the British. That's been Ireland's experience. But look at other cases abroad. Mass movements fizzle out. The smaller elitist groups have more staying power, more dedication. History is full of examples."

"Right enough. The twelve apostles springs to mind at once."

"Very funny."

"Well I'm only kidding. No offence. Actually they're good ideas. New arguments. But you didn't pick them up on the streets of Brayspont. And it's not the usual banter here in Casey's. Is this what Mr. Myles Flanaghan has been filling your head with?"

"His ideas make sense. The Irish as people have always been too easily divided. Too easily sold short. A dedicated revolutionary elite can avoid all the pitfalls of the mass movements of the past. United Ireland? We were never united at any time in our history. That's how a conqueror gets a hold, of course, over a divided people. And to maintain his position he has to keep the subject, the people, divided."

"What! The English guilty of perfidy, of divide and rule? They might do it out in India but I always thought they never needed it here. They simply suppressed discontent with sheer brutality. Or deported it on the prison ships to the ends of the earth."

"They used both Sean. Both. Divide and rule and downright brutality. What of the Ulster Protestants? They've always divided them from the rest of us."

"The Ulster Protestants. They're not Irish. Even say so themselves. Running about with Union Jacks and kissin' the arse of the King of England. How in God's name are they Irish? British settlers."

"They're here long enough to be Irish," Eamonn spoke into his glass as he made for another swallow, " only haven't found out yet, eh? And how about their mass movement? It's been successful enough. Sure seems to have the British Parliament by the balls at the minute."

More deep swallows of beer.

"Their cultural experience has been different. In every divided society there has to be someone benefiting from the division. They've been beneficiaries. They don't seek a revolution. They seek to thwart one. They need to maintain the status quo."

Eamonn banged his now empty pint glass on the table.

"I'm away to the bogs. I'm burstin' for a piss."

"Already?"

"It's a cold night ain't it? Your round."

Sean had Ma Casey refill the glasses. Returning to his seat he removed his great coat – the pub was now quite warm. The clamour in the pub grew. More patrons were arriving, all red faced and bright eyed from the cold. The ever present veil of tobacco smoke, garlanding the rafters grew thicker. Sean's attention was caught by the familiar figure of Mai Casey. She moved in her graceful effortless way towards the fire. She was carrying turf. The girl passed Sean and on reaching the fire went down on her haunches to stack the turf on the fire. The girl's slender, feminine form glowed warmly in the light of the fire. Sean, his elbow on the table, rested his chin on his hand, and gazed longingly at her. Mai turned and caught his admiring gaze. His wistful look was not lost on her. Her face lit up in a disarming smile.

"Would you never burn some decent coal on that fire Mai?" said Sean, "coal gives out a better heat."

"You're one cold fish Sean Maloney. I don't know what it'd take to warm you up."

"Oh now, I can think of a few things – besides coal and turf that is. But I suppose a turf fire'll do for now."

"Burn everything English but her coal. Who was it said so?"

"A bitter man."

"Mai!" Ma Casey bawled from the bar.

"I'd better be back helping mother."

With that Mai went back to the bar, her movement as silent and as graceful as any swan's. Again Sean found himself savouring the lovely outline of her small shoulders, narrow waist and her buttocks, showing firm and round beneath her skirt.

Just then a sudden chill gripped Sean. The front door opened and shut again quickly, but the icy coldness of the winter's night filled the pub. The closed door now framed a tall unfamiliar figure. The newcomer wore a navy great coat draped about his shoulders like a cloak, only the neck button was closed. He wore brown woolen trousers and leather riding boots. A broad brimmed felt hat cast his face in shadow, only a large ginger moustache was visible. In his right hand he held a walking cane.

An air of quiet descended upon the bar as its clientele turned to survey the newcomer. But the man seemed oblivious to their attentions, as though he were used to such. He shook the snow from his coat and approached the bar. Sean noticed that despite the walking cane there was no limp. Ma Casey was beckoned and a drink ordered – a glass of port. The stranger spoke with what Sean took to be and educated southern brogue. A Dubliner no doubt. As suddenly as it had stopped the conversation in the pub started again, Ma Casey's decision to serve the newcomer being taken by all to imply a certain acceptance if not a welcome. The relaxed noisy atmosphere resumed.

"Ah god it's damned cold in that fuckin'yard."

Sean turned to see Eamonn returned and taking his seat again. Eamonn took a mouthful of stout and continued, "you know what the fox said when he pissed in the snow."

Sean, again fixing his eyes on the newcomer at the bar, interrupted his friends casual banter. Tapping Eamonn on the shoulder Sean pointed.

"Now Eamonn. Would that by any chance be Mr Myles Flanaghan?"

"That's him."

Eamonn rose from his chair and went over to greet Flanaghan. After shaking hands the two stood talking quietly. Eamonn pointed in Sean's direction and ushered Flanaghan over to the table. Sean rose to his feet and extended his hand.

"Sean Maloney."

"Myles Flanaghan," came the reply, as the hat was removed, revealing a balding head of ginger hair, receding from the temples. His face was gaunt, pale and closely shaven. On his hawkish nose was perched a pair of steel-rimmed spectacles. Sean noticed his handshake was firm and ice cold. With a brief smile Flanaghan revealed a row of tobacco stained teeth. He smelled strongly of a curious mixture of tobacco, garlic and cheap soap.

The trio sat down. Flanaghan sat bolt upright in his chair, one arm extended toward the table and his glass of port, the other hand still grasped his walking cane, like some ancient potentate grasping his symbol of authority.

"Gentlemen," said Flanaghan, "my stay in Brayspont will be brief. I've booked into that charming old hotel across the square. What's the name – The Crown."

Flanaghan's voice was cold, affecting a friendly tone. "We're still laying the foundations of our organisation. We're strong in Dublin but weak in the provinces. This is where we hope that people like yourselves will help, especially in an area where the UVF seem so strong. Now your careers may soon take you to University in Dublin. If so you'll be just as welcome with us there."

"Myles," Sean interrupted, "Eamonn has just been talking of the importance of keeping the movement small and elitist.. Are you now talking of the movement expanding?"

"No. We're only expanding the basic network geographically. Numerically speaking we remain small. But we must be widespread, with roots amongst the people. If we were too big too soon the British could easily penetrate the movement. And the easiest way to destroy any movement is from within. No we stay small. When a truly revolutionary situation arises in this country then we'll be best poised to avail of it. Then we expand. Or perhaps give a lead might be better. Lead a mass movement of resistance to imperialism."

Flanaghan, with deliberate, sweeping movement of his hand, raised his glass and drank the last of his port. He then took out a gold cigarette case from his pocket and opened it.

"This revolutionary situation," said Sean, "how do you see it coming about for Ireland?"

Flanaghan did not reply at once, but pensively played with a cigarette, tapping its end gently on the table. Then on lighting the cigarette came the considered reply. "War must break out soon in Europe. It must. Such is the rivalry of the Imperialist powers. A war between heavyweights. A war of industialised nations, fielding armies the like of which has never been seen before. The Balkans is just a hint of what is to come. If England gets into difficulties then we can strike. An armed revolt by a few dedicated men can make a difference. The brutality of England's response will be the real spark. The spark that fires the lost nationalism of the Irish. Sacrifices will have to be made. Sacrifices are inevitable."

"What of the volunteers. The Irish volunteers I mean," said Sean.

"They'll be useful to a point. Soon they'll respond to the UVF. They will also arm."

Flanaghan drew again from his cigarette, which he held between his fingers like a throwing dart. Exhaling through his nose, he rose from the table and picked up his hat.

"Now gentlemen I'll bid you goodnight. I want to retire early. Good to have met you Sean. Goodnight Eamonn. We'll be in contact again."

Flanaghan put on his hat and moved toward the door with an exaggerated military stride, swinging his walking cane before him. Before opening the door he stopped, pulled up the lapels of his great coat, and adjusted his hat to bring the brim low over his forehead. He opened the door and walked out into the night. Sean tingled as the chill of the night air hit his face.

"Well what d'you think?" said Eamonn.

"A brief enough introduction," said Sean, "believes in coming straight to the point. No small talk. Certainly a man of firmly held ideas."

"Convictions," Eamonn corrected him, "firmly held convictions."

"Ok then," Sean continued, "call it what you will. But he sure has a way of making you feel uneasy, downright uncomfortable in fact."

"Listen Sean. The Myles Flanaghans of this world were not born to make people feel comfortable. They were born to topple empires. That man is one hundred per cent rebel. He's a total nationalist. To him the very notion of compromise is an anathema. In politics Sean, you'll no doubt meet more of the likes of Myles Flanaghan."

"Politics is that what we call it? I thought politics was raising hell at the town council meeting once a month. This is war isn't it? Or a revolution at least? Let's finish our drinks and go home."

"What! Just like that. After such a brilliantly interesting evening," Eamonn slurred.

"Fucks sake! Ok!" said Sean, "let's finish our drinks. Go home, and await our revolutionary situation."

"Right!" bellowed Eamonn, "I'll raise me glass to that!" He then banged his glass down on the table with sufficient force to smash it, and bring an embarrassed hush over Casey's bar. Eamonn stared back at his amazed peers.

"Well fuck that anyway."

November 1914

The European war had erupted in August. It seemed that the troubles of Eastern Europe had suddenly and inexplicably come to Ireland. There was much excitement in the country. The Ulster Protestants in a show of determined loyalty to king and Empire enlisted with a wild enthusiasm. Nationalists rushed to the colours also. Promises of Home Rule and a sympathy for 'Poor little Catholic Belgium' probably played their part. No doubt many, Protestant and Catholic alike, saw opportunities for adventure, heroism and simply needing the 'King's shilling.'

In Brayspont the progress of the armies across Belgium and Northern France was followed with a keen interest. No one had even begun to comprehend the scale of the slaughter.

The morning was cold and misty. In Newquay train station people sat huddled near the ticket office. Among them was Robert McBride. He sat on a bench with a kit bag at his feet.

"You off to join up then? Answering the call?"

Robert turned to meet a tall freckled faced youth whom he took to be not much older than himself. The youth sucked firmly on a rolled up cigarette.

"That's right," replied Robert, "I'm for Eniskillen."

"Me too. We'll have company on the train. Those two."

He gestured over his shoulder at two youths sitting further

down the platform. Their conversation was animated and distinctly punctuated with the 'F' word.

"Two good guys. Sean Hennessy and Dalton. Mick Dalton – all he ever gets is Dalton. Don't mind the 'effing' though – he's got a heart of corn."

"Robert McBride." Robert offered his hand. The newcomer gave it a firm manly shake, clenching the cigarette in a row of smiling teeth.

"Willie Scott. Is this for King and Empire then?"

"Well I suppose so. Haven't thought it all through yet."

Robert was surprised at his own evasiveness. He was a reluctant recruit and he knew it."

"Me – I suppose it's family. My folks have always joined up. Mad fools all of 'em"

"Now those two," Scott nodded at Hennessy and Dalton, "their hoping Redmond will make good on his promises – Home Rule. Can't please everyone I suppose."

The screech of a train whistle interrupted. Hissing and clanking, the Locomotive emerged from the early morning gloom. Robert was glad of the reprieve from the politics. But he felt relieved – he'd met friends.

"Enniskillen here we come," said Willie.

"France here we come," said Robert.

Then followed the rousing strain of "Fare thee well Enniskillen."

Further up the platform Hennessy and Dalton had broken into song.

Spring 1915

Sean's acquaintance with Andreena was growing
stronger. They would meet and stroll in the
Brayspont town park or along its seafront-
promenade. The town's railway link would help fill the town's
tearooms and pubs at weekends. The promenade, with its
fountains and open-air seawater baths was their special place.
The couple became adept at losing themselves in the crowds
away from the prying eyes of family and friends. Soon a
different crowd would beckon.

Another relationship had been growing stronger –Taidg
and Mary. When Mary left her employment with the
McBrides she made her way south to Dublin – initially to stay
with relations and find new employment. Taidg followed soon
after.

It was on one of their afternoon strolls in the park that
Andreena informed Sean of her intention of going south –
initially not quite all the way to Dublin. She would go to her
Uncle's estate (Yes! Yet another McBride estate) Sean was
invited to join her there. The provincial, arcadian world of
Brayspont would soon be in the past.

"Nursing! Am I hearing things?" Sean exclaimed with
certain teasing delight.

They were sitting on the steps of the town Park's Band
stand.

"And why not? You think I'm not fit for it?" replied Andreena.

"Well – I always thought grand ladies didn't nurse."

"Don't you grand lady me. Lady yes but forget the grand bit. Besides -wasn't Florence Nightingale a grand Lady?"

"Ah so that's it," said Sean, "this war. You're thinking of going to Fance?"

"Could all be over by the time I'm finished training."

"Doesn't look like it. All over by Christmas indeed."

A sudden chill wind ended the conversation. Sensing an oncoming rain shower the couple left the park and made their way to the town centre. Here they parted . As always there was no indiscreet escort home. Sean wasn't dismayed at Andreena's news. Indeed she seem to enthral him all the more.

May 1915

ndreena's uncle's estate proved to be every bit as beautiful as she had said. When they arrived by its lake the sky was clear and the calm water was shimmering in the brilliant summer sunshine. The trees were in their full deep green livery. The whin bushes were ablaze with their fiery yellow flowers. Sean had met Andreena as planned by the old wooden gate lodge. From there they took a secluded path through the woods to the boathouse. As the path neared the lakeside, the older sycamore trees gave way to much younger willows, silver birches and flowering cherries. The late spring storms had strewn the blossoms about the pathway and over the floor of the wood.

The pair walked slowly, deliberately through the carpet of petals. Scan wore dark cotton trousers and a matching waistcoat. He also wore a tie and a stiff white collar. Closely shaven – his hair was meticulously groomed. Andreena wore a long slim fitting cream skirt and a plain white blouse. Her red hair was tied up in a pony tail revealing her slender and beautiful neck. She wore a broad brimmed straw hat and carried a parasol – she twirled its ivory handle continuously.

"I've put a picnic basket in the boat," she said.

"My – we are organised."

"Some fruit, some cake and a bottle of wine.

Andreena sat in the rear of the boat – the parasol over her

right shoulder. To Sean the sunlight cascading about her made her glow in an unreal celestial light. He strained at the oars as the boat cut through the still water like a steel blade through silk. The only sounds were the rippling of the water and the creaking of the rollicks as the oars dipped and rose. Sean stopped. Two swans, disturbed by the boats approach, took to the air. With much honking and splashing the birds raced low over the lake and gradually climbed skyward.

"They're beautiful," Andreena murmured.

"Yes indeed. That island over to the left, with the old ruin, what's it like?"

"Very overgrown but there's a clearing near the ruin. Uncle claims the ruin was a monastery."

"Ruined by Henry VIII no doubt. He ripped off all the monasteries. He was a bloody thief as well as a dirty old man."

"Bigot," Andreena laughed, "actually my Uncle blames the Vikings."

"He would I suppose."

Sean turned the boat and pulled steadily for the island. On gaining the shallows he climbed out and beached the boat. He helped Andreena out and after removing the picnic basket secured the boat by pulling it up onto the shore.

The clearing Andreena spoke of was secluded – surrounded by rhododendron, its lavender flowers were in full bloom. The floor of the clearing was covered with lush long grass and wild flowers. It was here that they made love.

★ ★ ★

December 1915

Outside the distant dull thuds of trench mortars punctured the stillness. The calm inside the dugout made a curious indeed surreal contrast.

The light of bursting flares would momentarily illumine the doorway. Eerie shafts of light intruded on the grotto like intimacy of the dugout.

Dalton, his face etched with determination, drew hard on his cigarette.

Slowing exhaling he seemed in an inner agony.

"You know Robbie. What really gets to me most – is not the dying. Nor even mutilation. It's being buried alive under this lot. Direct hit. We're already in the tomb."

"Try not to think of it so much."

"I try not to. But can't do that all the time. Living like this – man can't but think of his end."

The men started as they became aware of a presence outside. The canopy parted and a crouching figure entered. The newcomer straightened up and the lamp light shone on the face of Leutenant Dawson, the Padre. The men relaxed again.

"Evening McBride – Dalton."

"Evening Padre."

"I'll have some of that wine you're not supposed to have."

"Sorry Padre. We've just polished off the last of it."

"Not to worry. Brought me own source of solace along."

The Padre pulled a silver flask from inside his tunic.

"Spare me an empty mug?"

"Here y'go Padre," said Dalton proffering a tin mug.

"Now men. Whenever a padre arrives most of you think 'trouble'. And yes part of our job is to be the bearing of bad tidings. Well this evening's no exception I'm afraid. It's your friend Smith.

Robert started in horror. "My God he's not…?"

"Dead? No. But might as well be if he's caught. Done a runner. Deserted."

"Oh shit!"

"He'd been brooding a lot recently. Quiet. Keeping to himself. Hard to spot that sort of thing till it's too late. Mates can't spot everything. We're all clammed up with our own fears I suppose."

"When did it happen?" asked Robbie.

"Yesterday. Donned civy dress and all. Gendarmes been alerted. They'll catch him for sure. Sorry to say that."

"Sorry to say that," whispered Dalton. "Shouldn't a King's officer be glad to catch a deserter."

"I'm God's servant first Lad. Try not to be bitter. You will be angry when they catch him. But don't be bitter. Bitterness will destroy more than shot 'n' shell."

"Sorry Padre. Wasn't meaning to get at you. Just it's this awful mess of war."

The conversation stopped. The men had finished their drinks. The padre opened his cigarette case and offered each man a smoke. He lit up himself and the lamplight was soon garlanded in thin wispy trails of smoke.

From the distance the thudding of the trench mortars intruded again.

"Believe you'd a spot of bother down here today."

"Bother? Yea . You could call it that," said Dalton."All over a bunch of navies."

"Navies? But How?"

"Well these navies came down. Shoring up the communication trench. Ballockses. Fritz heard them and must and figured we were diggin' a mine. Shelled us for half an hour. Eight dead. What a mess!"

"Well yes I always hear about the lads that get posted. Look men I'll be off. Keep in contact. I'll let you know what I hear on poor old Smith."

"Evenin' Padre."

Dalton put his hand on Robbie's shoulder.

"Maybe it'll turn out ok. He could get to Spain. Never know."

"No chance. When you that homesick you'll not be headin' the other way."

Dalton moved to the doorway and pulled aside the canopy.

"Well – if that's not all we need!"

"What's that?"

"Snow. It's startin' to snow."

★ ★ ★

The frozen, lunar landscape was glowing with the dying afterglow of the sunset. Earlier, even the barbed wire looked cheerful, covered in icicles that sparkled in the winter sunshine.

Then the dusk gathered and the gloom deepened. A fogbank was gathering and would soon cover the German positions. Robbie was using a trench periscope to watch the line. But visibility was poor. Dalton sat near him, warming his mitted hands on a tea mug.

"Not a cheap nor chirp. Bastards have been quiet all day."

"So why complain. Fritz enjoys Christmas too. Christmas trees was a German custom you know."

"Last year they sang carols. Our side joined in. Winded up playing Football."

"Who won?"

"They did. Two – nil."

"No Chance this year. Bloody officers."

"Waste o' time. Packin' this in for a bit."

"Get yourself a tea. Maybe Fritz will sing some carols instead."

Later in the dugout Irish could hear the Germans celebrate. A harmonica started up. "Stille Nacht Heilige Nacht."

The moon rose and spread its silver sheen over the snowscape. In the trenches the men shivered under their tin hats and balaclavas. They thought of home and sang of love and peace.

★ ★ ★

The day after Christmas Robbie again met Leutenant Dawson.

"They've got him," announced the Padre.

"Was picked up yesterday. Quayside in Calais above all places. Heading for home. Civy dress and carrying a suitcase."

"They'll shoot him?"

"Yes I'm afraid so. Set an example and all that."

"Poor bloody fool, said Robbie."What'll they tell his folks?"

"Killed in action."

"Noble of them."

"Now Robbie remember what I said. Nothing we can do. Bitterness is going to do no one any good."

The padre produced his flask and two mugs. They sat talking and sipping brandy.

★ ★ ★

The court martial was held the next day at the regimental HQ. This was in a substantial red bricked farmhouse several miles to the rear. Dawson was there and so were most of the officers. A junior officer was assigned to the unfortunate Smith's defence. A mood of grim resignation consumed most of the men. Fatalism was now endemic after seventeen months of carnage. For most, a bitter charade was unfolding. The inevitable sentence was passed and scheduled for the following morning.

That night Robert's company were withdrawn from the line to witness the "justice." The dawn was cold, grey and misty. The men were in a grim mood; stern, ashen faced, as though about to go 'over the top.' Before the farmyard wall a pile of sandbags had been made ready. Before this was a single wooden post. The post even had butcher's S-hooks affixed so as to arrest the condemned man's fall. Smith was soon led out. He was sobbing wretchedly.

Lt Dawson walked beside him reading from the Bible.

Robbie fixed his eyes on then grey sky above and stood rigidly in line. Inside, he was in turmoil, but determined to keep his eyes skyward. He could hear Smith sobbing and the Padre's praying. Form a nearby wood rooks cawed their dawn chorus. Then came the shouted commands and the drawing of rifle bolts; then the brutal crash of the volley. A momentary, stunned silence – then the rooks soared skyward screaming in protest. Robbie followed their flight through tear filled eyes. More shouted orders and back to the trenches.

February 1916

Sean stood before an old church yard. The sky was overcast and a light freezing drizzle was falling. Sean shivered, hunching his shoulders and burying his hands deep in the pockets of his greatcoat.

"Flanaghan's a bloody eccentric. But what the fuck's he at now? Hauling me all the way down here just for a chat," Sean grumbled aloud as he opened the churchyard gate. The wet gravel slipped and crunched under his shoes as he walked up the pathway. He tried the church door – it was locked. He made his way round to the rear of the church.

The wind gently swayed the great trees of the graveyard. The tombstones stood tall and sombre against the greyness of the sky. Walking amongst them, Sean would occasionally stop to read an inscription or observe a date. His cynical mood left him unmoved. 'How useless,' he thought, 'useless slabs of stone for what? To mark the transitoriness of human existence. The last resting places of people who once laughed, loved, fought, ate, worked, got drunk – and died. Yet there had to be more. There had to be. Or why was he, Sean Maloney now in this graveyard, but to talk of a great enterprise.'

Then Sean saw Flanaghan. He was seated beneath a willow tree. His broad felt hat pulled low over his face, his wet storm cape draped dramatically about him like a tent. 'Flanaghan,' thought Sean, 'definitely had feeling for theatre.'

"Myles," said Sean, "what takes you here amongst the dead?"

"The dead don't hear very well, In fact they don't hear at all. I'm growing wary of pubs and tea rooms."

Paranoia was setting in.

"You know Sean this is a very interesting old place. Handel was once the organist here. Worked on the 'Messiah' in this very church, so I'm told. And the vaults beneath the church contain some very unusual burials. The air in the vaults seems to preserve the corpses. Two of the burials are of patriots of the 1798."

"Myles I'm sure you haven't taken me out here just for a history lesson."

"Well yes. I suppose I have. Because that's what you and I – and our likes – are all about – history. Very soon, you and I, and our generation of rebels, must pass into history. Only this time as successful rebels. They say Emmet is buried in the churchyard. Myth? But then so much of inspiration is derived from myth. I forget the exact quote, but didn't Emmet speak of his epithet being written by a future generation. Let's hope we're the men to write it."

"All very well Myles. But neither you nor I are martyrs. Patriots yes."

Flanaghan was silent for a moment. He stood playing with the ends of his moustache with his long bony fingers. It was a pose of his which was now familiar to Sean. Something profound was to follow. The wistful look left Flanaghan's eyes and the sinister, lizard look was again on his face.

"We shall rise soon. This war does not go well for the British. Soon the Titans will fall exhausted. And we must strike while the rod is hot. But we've missed you Sean. We haven't seen you in months. Your dedication is as strong as ever I hope?"

"Playing toy soldiers was never for me Myles. When the real thing comes I'll be there."

"Ah! Spoken like a true backwoodsman. A reservist!" Flanaghan smiled a thin toothy smile of triumph, "Well now Sean. We'll be calling on the reserves very soon. Here take this."

Flanaghan pulled aside his cape and drew out a pistol. It was a German Mauser. Holding it by the barrel he thrust its butt into Sean's hand. Sean looked in awe at its pristine blue metal. It was heavy and cold in his palm. He and Flanaghan eyed each other for a moment, their gaze steady and stern. Then Flanaghan placed a reassuring hand on Sean's shoulder.

"Keep it safe my friend for believe me, the day is near."

Together they turned and walked from the graveyard. At the gates Flanaghan again admonished Sean for his absence. Then they parted. Sean hurried home. As he arrived back at his lodgings the daylight was fast fading. The streetlights were by now reflecting on the wet streets.

That night Sean examined his new charge. He emptied the magazine and put the bullets in the bottom of his locker. Then he left the gun on his bedside table, under a candle. He looked in fascination at its sinister deadly shape and wondered at its awesome potential – a new, cold, cold mistress.

April 1916

"**m**ornin' missus. What are you doin' out an' about this mornin' of all mornings?"

Taidg addressed a thin, stoned faced old lady dressed in black. Her glasses perched determinedly on the end of her button nose, her mouth was thin and puckered and she smelt of camphor. "An' why shouldn't I be out and about young man? Those foolish shinners shall not deter me. Are you open for business?"

"Well – yes and no. That is to say we're not exactly open and we're not exactly closed. We're in the process of closing up. We're not for hangin' about to get ourselves shot. Are we Molly?"

"No indeed Taidg," came a soft voice from the back of the shop, and then even softer, "bloody sure we're not."

The old lady scowled indignantly. "I would like a quarter pound of tea please."

"Very well missus. Here you go. One quarter pound of tea. A rebellion just wouldn't be a rebellion without a cuppa tea."

The old lady fumbled in her purse.

"That's okay," said Taidg, who was by now getting impatient, "you can pay next time you're in dear. Now I'm closing up, sharpish, thank you."

Taidg gently ushered her out.

"Auld orange bitch!" called Molly from the back.

"Now darlin', people are entitled to their opinions y'know. Even is she is …"

"An auld orange bitch."

"An auld orange bitch then."

Molly laughed. Then suddenly her mood changed. She was worried. Her voice trembled as she spoke.

"I'm hurrying on home Taidg. Just in case anything really does happen. I know some of the shinners. Nice boys – but they're hotheads. A handful of hotheads against the great British Empire. I wouldn't give much for their chances."

"Hotheads y'say. The ones I know wouldn't qualify for that title I think. Ice water in the veins. That type. Well not to worry. You go on. I'll take the fruit an' veg' stands in. Then I'll pull the shutters and lock up."

As he finished speaking Taidg reached out and gently touched her cheek in a reassuring gesture. Molly was looking very beautiful. Her complexion was pale and clear. Her cheeks were gently flushed, her lips cherry red, and her curling auburn hair fell magnificently about her shoulders. She moved close to Taidg, so close he felt the warmth of her breath and the rapid rise and fall of her bosom. Then she kissed him. When she withdrew, Taidg, at first bewildered, then delighted, gazed longingly at her. Her blue eyes had a distant far away look.

"Hurry Taidg. Take care. Get home quickly. Your wife'll need you now."

Quickly she turned and hurried out. Taidg stood for a minute gazing at the doorway, then, continued to get ready. A sudden shattering volley of shots made him freeze in terror. The volley was followed by yet another. Then came a ragged burst of shots and panicky unintelligible shouting. Silence followed – eerie and piercing. Taidg forced himself to move to the front of the shop. Looking up and down the street at first he saw no one. Then, looking again, barely a hundred yards from the shop, a woman's body lay in the roadway. Taidg at once recognized Molly's green skirt, shawl and white blouse.

He raced to her side. She lay face down. Gently but quickly he lifted her, turning her over and cradling her in his arms. Her beautiful head rolled lifelessly backwards and her now still, glassy blue eyes gazed skywards. Beneath her left breast a dark red patch was spreading. Taidg shook uncontrollably. Tears welled up in his eyes as he held Molly even more tightly.

"Bastards! Bastards!" he screamed.

He sobbed deeply and painfully. He gathered her in his arms and carried her back to the shop. At the doorway he staggered drunkenly. A sudden pain burned his shoulder. He stood swaying, grasping Molly's body in disbelief. Taidg never heard the next shot. The bullet struck him in the middle of the back and passed through his heart. He collapsed. He and Molly crashed into the fruit boxes as they fell. The fruit spilled over their lifeless bodies and rolled into the gutter.

★ ★ ★

The village had an uneasy air that morning. Sean sensed it. Uneasy himself, he felt the tension in the air about him. In the main street he found Tobin's pub. He went inside and ordered a glass of whiskey. From under his bushy, smoky grey eyebrows Tobin glared suspiciously at Sean.

"You've heard the news from Dublin?" Tobin rasped.

"I've heard there's been a spot of bother."

"Bother! It's plenty of bother. The bloody shinners have taken the G.P.O. Tried to take the castle as well b'God. Shootin' in the streets an' everything. It'll do no good I tell you. The bloody English'll come down hard on us. Always have in this country."

Sean decided not to respond. Conveniently the old man shuffled off to the lower end of the bar muttering as he went. Then the door opened and the stale air of the bar gave way to a gust of fresh air. Silhouetted in the hard sunlight was Myles Flanaghan (if ever a man knew how to make an entrance). With an arrogant strut he approached the bar. Eamonn also emerged from the sunlight and shut the door. The soft nether light of the pub proved gentler on the eyes.

"Really Sean. At this hour of the day. And us with so much in front of us, " Fanaghan spoke in an admonishing tone.

"It's only a small whiskey. Besides. It's better to be in here than to be stuck outside attracting attention. This is quite a small village y'know?"

"Gentlemen?" Tobin called from the back.

"Nothing thank you," replied Eamonn, "we're just meeting our friend then we'll be off."

"The far side of the street," said Sean, "a British patrol."

"Yes we've seen them," said Eamonn, "not much of a patrol – an officer, a driver and two cops."

"Hardly a patrol at all," said Flanaghan, "they're our ticket into the City. The trains have stopped running. So we're commandeering their car. Our first act in the rebellion. If we're quick – it should not be a problem. Have you got your pistol?"

"Yes." The colour drained from Sean's face as he spoke.

"Now Sean, it has all started. The moment of truth Sean. Remember – the matador?"

"I'll be okay! I'll be okay!"

"Good. Good. The officer seems to have stepped into that tea house. I shall go and have some tea. Then I'll wait for you to cross the road to the newsagents. As soon as you're in position I'll take the officer. Soon as you hear my shots you'll open fire from the newsagents, Eamonn from this side. Got it?"

Sean swallowed hard and blurted out, "Got it!"

Flanaghan after pausing to brief Eamonn, went outside and strode boldly across the road. The soldier and the two constables saw no threat in the bespectacled, aristocratic figure approaching them. Flanaghan, passing unchallenged, entered the tea parlour.

Now Sean moved. Nodding quietly to Eamonn he left the darkness of the pub for the sunshine outside. He crossed the road. His blood pounded in his eardrums. His throat tightened with fear. His hands in his pockets, one clutching his pistol, sweated profusely.

"The moment of truth. The moment of truth." Flanaghan's words echoed in his head. He reached the newsagents and it happened. Two shots rent the silence of the sleepy village. A moment of eerie silence, then a chorus of screams. The driver and the constables had barely reacted when Eamonn's fusillade of shots cut down the constables. The driver dived for cover seeking to retrieve a weapon from the car. Sean, wide-eyed with disbelief acted. Drawing his pistol he fired twice. The soldier reeled back from the car, collapsing onto the pavement. He held himself up on one arm as he fought for life. Another shot rang out. The driver pitched forward onto the pavement and was still. Sean now saw that Flanaghan had emerged from the tea parlour a smoking pistol in his hand. He yelled at the two younger men.

"Grab their weapons," get the car started! We've got to get out of here! To Dublin! To Dublin!" he shrieked in triumph.

Chaos reigned in the village. People screamed. Somewhere a woman cried in a tortured unearthly wail. An old man started shouting.

"Up the rebels! Up the rebels!"

Someone else shouted, "Murder!"

April 1916 – The Rising

Sean blinked open his eyes. The light hurt. Slowly he twisted his body round and lay on the flat of his back. Straining his eyes he focused his gaze on the ceiling. His side ached due to his cramped sleeping position.

Across the shuttered room Flanaghan slept soundly, his body curled in a pre-natal crouch, his head on a satchel. Beside the window, spread low on a mattress the young volunteer still kept watch. His face was lined with fatigue – rivulets of sweat washed trails down his smoke blackened face.

"All still quiet," asked Sean.

"Of course it is," replied the young rebel, "otherwise you and your friend would've had a noisy awakin'. I suppose the Tommies need their rest just like ourselves."

A crash of falling rubble sounded behind them.

"What the fuck was that?!

"Falling bricks. That's probably what's roused ya from slumberland. The lads have got some axes and a crowbar. They're battering holes in the walls between the houses. If we can get far enough down this terrace, then just maybe we can break out. S'matter a fact that noise is coming from three houses down. Working like moles, the lads are."

"Great," said Sean softly, "but the bloody British. They ain't fuckin' deaf y'know. They're easily within earshot. They'll hear that racket for sure."

"Well. Who's got a better idea then?"

"Oh I know. I know. But the British are tightening their grip all round. They'll soon penetrate this area and take us for keeps."

"Well that hasn't happened yet. Y'know we're lucky. In the rest of the city our lads are just holding isolated strongpoints – completely surrounded. At least we've got some chance of slipping away. Get somewhere to hide. Pass ourselves off as civilians."

"Madness," muttered Sean, "sheer madness. Penning ourselves up like this for the British to surround and pound into submission."

An icy voice cut through the room, "Military victory is not what this is all about. Military victory was never possible nor was it ever intended," Flanaghan had awoken.

"Well Myles it sure beats losing."

"Who says this is losing. Sean – I told you. Our victory will only come from the bloody crushing of this rising. Phoenix – like out nation will arise from these very ashes."

"Hold it," said the young rebel, "the Tommies are up to something. They're moving about over there."

Flanaghan and Sean roused themselves and crawled closer to the wall, to take up a position. The sudden report from a Lee-Enfield was instantly followed by the smashing of another of the room's red bricks, showering dust about the room. The rebels tensed and crouched lower.

"I see the ballocks," said the young rebel, "and I've got a line on him."

Taking careful aim the rebel Mauser cracked. A loud scream issued from down the street followed by a crash of glass.

"He took a dive."

The British reply was furious. Their position erupted in rifle fire. The rebels were showered with bullets, screaming and whining as they ricocheted. Rapidly the small room filled with blinding, choking dust. Then a bullet found its mark. The young rebel screamed as he was hurled across the room, his back arched, his head snapped back as his body contorted with the impact. His face twisted in pain – his mouth opened for yet another scream. He writhed in agony on the floor. Sean scrambled over to him, putting his arm around him to support his back.

As suddenly as it had started the British fusillade ceased. It was as though the scream of the wounded man told them they had had their revenge.

"Where's he hit?" called Flanaghan.

"In the shoulder. Drilled clean through. We've got to get him out of here."

"To where?"

"To the next house. C'mon. Into the hallway. The lads have broken into the next few houses."

"Sean! Sean!"

It was Eamonn calling.

"Are you alright?"

"Yes. But this lad's been hit. Stay where you are. We're coming."

"Well have to crawl all the way," said Flanaghan, "we'll have to drag him."

"What's your name?" asked Flanaghan, of the barely conscious youth.

"Flynn. Flynn." he whispered.

"Very well young Flynn. Hang on. We're going to get you out."

Crawling all the way, and dragging the wounded Flynn, they wormed their way from room to room and from house to house. Sean would go through the holes in the walls first, supporting Flynn's head and shoulders as Flanaghan, gripping his lower torso, pushed him through. Flynn weak and barely conscious managed to push on his legs. Eventually they rejoined Eamonn and his companions who had by now broken into their fourth house.

No sooner had they done so than an English accent sounded from down the street.

"Irish! Irish! Alright Irish the games up. Come out with your hands up. We've brought up a field gun. So help me we'll use it. We'll blast you out."

"They're bluffing," said Eamonn.

"Don't think so," said Flanaghan.

"C'mon Irish," came another shout, "throw down your weapons and come on out. We'll treat you decent."

"Liars!"

"What are we gonna do? We can't trust them."

"Fuck them. I know what I'm gonna do," said Eamonn, "I'm gonna keep tunnellin' out of here." Picking up a crowbar he recommenced battering at the house wall. A steady ringing sounded at the bar impacted on the stone.

A huge explosion shook the house. It was follower by the sound of falling timbers and bricks. Outside a huge cloud of smoke began to billow up the street. The shell had struck the end house.

"B'jasus – the weren't bluffin'. Were they?" said Eamonn.

"No indeed," said Flanaghan. "He who fights and runs away, lives to fight another day. Anybody know one about surrendering?"

"No Myles. But how about this? He who surrenders has no fuckin'choice."

With that Sean moved to the front door and threw it open. He threw his rifle out first – it clattered noisily as it hit the road. Hands held high Sean marched out into the brilliant sunshine. He could immediately see the effect of the shell – it had completely destroyed the house that until a few minutes ago he, Flanaghan and Flynn had been defending.

Sean squinted in the bright sunshine and through the thinning smoke he could see the khaki clad figures of the enemy approaching. Their fixed bayonets glinted in the sun. A tall dignified figure with officer's epaulettes strode forward. His pistol was still in his holster – he carried only a riding crop. He stood there with all the majestic arrogance of the master race beholding an underling. But Sean felt no sense of inferiority. He also stood proudly, indeed magnificently in the sunshine of the fine April day. Then suddenly the full significance of Flanaghan's words hit him. This was not about military victory.

"And the others?" enquired the officer. "They're coming," Sean replied coolly, then he shouted, "c'mon out lads!"

Flanaghan emerged, walking with his usual swagger, unbowed in defeat. Eamonn and his companion followed assisting the wounded Flynn. Gently Flynn was lowered to the pavement.

"Very well," bayed the officer, "leave the wounded man. Our orderlies will see to him. The rest of you move out."

Quickly the Irish were surrounded by the bayonet wielding soldiers. With a certain amount of prodding with bayonets and digging with rifle butts the Irish were marched down the street. They passed the British position as they turned into a side street. As they marched they saw the field gun which had been their downfall – in itself, a potent symbol of the great enemy they had just fought.

Rounding the corner the prisoners met a despairing sight. Along the length of the street rebels were standing under armed guard. British soldiers stood in the middle of the roadway. Bayonets were fixed and menacing a group of Citizen Army volunteers and civilians caught up in the confusion of the street fighting. But many were genuine rebels. Sean recognised quite a few.

Sean and his friends were made to stand in line with the others. From there they could clearly see the activity in a builder's yard opposite. The yard had been commandeered as a field hospital. Through the open gates could be seen the rows of wounded civilians, British and Citizen Army. To one side was a military ambulance. Several men were able to sit up. Others lay on stretchers or rough wooden pallets. Others were being tended by orderlies, nurses and local women volunteers. Groans of agony were clearly audible as was a low pathetic whimpering. In one corner of the yard, was a row of covered bodies – the draped, bloodied sheets giving a limited dignity to those who had lost their fight for life.

"Move 'em out! Move the prisoners out!" a British NCO bawled at the top of his voice.

Menacingly the guards moved forward and with much pushing, jostling and threatening with bayonets, moved their wards down the street. Once moving the procession assumed a wearied, unhurried pace. Both prisoners and guards were exhausted by the fighting of the last week. On both sides there seemed an overwhelming acceptance of the fact of the surrender – the rebellion, the Easter Rebellion, was over. Yet it was but only one act of a long drama. The fact that the final act had yet to be written, was far from the minds of these weary men.

The rebels walked with bowed heads, shoulders drooping, at a shuffling pace. The British walked almost complacently at their sides. Moving towards the centre of the city the devastation wrought by the British artillery became obvious. Shell scarred buildings, shattered windows and the pervasive smell of burning. It was now that the rebels came under the attention of Dublin's infuriated citizens.

"Ya bastards!" called a toughened old woman from an upper window.

"Bloody murdering scum!" a young woman suddenly spat – *at Flanaghan!*

Flanaghan froze. The spit caught the lenses of his glasses. His countenance whitened. Slowly, with much deliberation, he removed his glassed and wiped the lenses with a kerchief. Then he moved off – his outraged pride visible in every determined stride.

Then from behind Sean someone screamed. A rock had struck home. The man's comrades caught him as he fell and struggled to keep him on his feet.

"Bastards!"

"Fuckin' rebel cunts!"

A scuffle broke out, as several bystanders descended on the group of men. The British sentries moved to intervene, striving to separate the melee. In the tumult Sean saw his opportunity. He knew he would have to move quickly. Carelessly, the British had neglected to search him when he surrendered – perhaps throwing down his rifle looked sufficiently resigned. They had not removed his Mauser. It was still crammed down his waist band, and this was concealed by his pullover. With his civilian clothing he would slip away. He must. His mind raced. Now or never. Quickly he joined the jostling crowd, and began to work his way round the other side – away from the sentries. Glancing all about him he began to move away. He'd slip into a doorway and hide. But where? Where was his chance?

The shattered front of a looted butcher's shop provided the answer he sought. Behind him the tumult was subsiding. In the porchway he felt the broken glass crunch under his feet as he tried the locked door. The owner must have returned to secure the premises – already light planking had been nailed criss-cross over the door's window.

Sean's pulse raced. His forehead suddenly streamed with sweat.

"What now?"

His hand now gripping the Mauser's butt firmly, he stood back. He kicked high and hard. It was enough. Quickly he pulled away a section of planking and slipped in his right hand and felt for a bolt. In a few seconds he was in.

He stood in the gloom of the shop, his back against a wall. His left hand was still grasping the Mauser. Outside the prisoners had moved on – only a few of the crowd remained, arguing furiously.

Looking about the shop, Sean observed that it had been

recently tidied. In a corner, beneath the scrubbed wooden chopping blocks was a pile of bloodied sawdust strewn with glass fragments. Opposite, the s-hooks hung devoid of their usual fare. Still on the wall, inspite of the looters, was an array of knives, cleavers and saws.

"How did you get in here you thieving scum?"

Sean turned to see a tall, burly man, with a slab of a red face, glaring at him. He advanced menacingly, the jowls of his cheeks shaking as he came.

"Stay where you are," Sean hissed, pulling out the Mauser.

The man stopped. Wary of the danger, his temper cooled.

"So. You'd shoot me too. A fine liberator you'd be."

"What do you mean?"

"You got my brother shot. Didn't ya? Didn't ya? And now I suppose its me?"

"What happened to your brother? How'd he get hit?"

"British patrol opened fire on him. Thought he was one of your lot. He's lying upstairs. Doctor's with him."

"Were there any Irish forces in the area at the time?"

"Yes. Nearby."

"Nearby? Just nearby? Was your brother with them?"

"No."

"Was he armed?"

"Course not."

"Well now. There's a fine piece of twisted thinking. There's a rebellion. The British send their imbecile army to crush it. They've been shooting Irish civilians on sight – one of them, your brother. So you blame the rebels."

"You started it didn't ya?"

"Oh, for God's sake. Well I'm not arguing any further. Fact

is mister, you're gonna help this particular rebel whether you like it or not. Now move! Upstairs!"

Keeping the man covered with his pistol, they went upstairs. In a small room at the back of the house a man lay in bed sleeping. His head was covered with a bloodied bandage. His torso also was bound in bloodied bandages. At a bedside table, beneath a picture of Christ, an elderly man was packing a doctor's case. At the sight of Sean brandishing a pistol the old man froze momentarily. Looking only mildly perturbed the old man continued his packing. He spoke quietly.

"May I be so bold as to enquire what's going on?"

"Was in the shop below –"

"I'd have thought that's obvious," Sean cut in, "I'm on the run and you're gonna help me."

"Don't be so sure of that. I've seen a lot of bloodshed these past few days. I myself am very much in the autumn of life. I'm not afraid. Threats won't get you too far."

The display of sang froid left Sean unnerved. He had not expected this. A week after living with the supremacy of brute force was already conditioning him. With the Doctor's next words he breathed more easily.

"Nevertheless. Help you need – help you'll get." Then turning to the butcher said, "We'd better cooperate with him. Bring him a change of clothes – your brother is about his size."

The butcher hesitated, a sullen look on his face.

"Well go on man! He's holding the gun. Do as he says."

The butcher shuffled out into the next room leaving Sean and the doctor alone with the unconscious patient. The Doctor was a tall thin man in a tweed suit. A gold watch and chain hung from his waistcoat. His grey hair was thinning on top and was long and disheveled at the temples and back. He pushed his gold-rimmed glasses onto his forehead and began to rub the corner of his eyes with his thumb and index finger. He looked exhausted.

"Actually young man – I'm rather in sympathy with you and your reckless colleagues. But you've got to understand your situation. Your rebellion comes in the middle of a great war in which many of Ireland's young men, however misguided, are fighting. All this to so many seems like a stab in the back. Oh I know, I know, England's difficulty Ireland's opportunity. But the city has suffered terribly these past few days, and oh how it has suffered. The ordinary people are blaming you. I'm afraid the people are not so much roused against the British as against you and your friends. Not everyone has your lofty ideals."

"So you class yourself as a patriot also?"

"And why not? You shinners hardly have a monopoly on it do you?"

"Look doctor. I'm sure you and I can have this out some other time. Can you get me out of here?"

"When you get this change of clothing you can come with me. I have a second briefcase you can carry it. You'll look just like a junior colleague or a medical student. That should get you past the British patrols. I'd advise you to dispose of that pistol though. I can't guarantee the British won't stop and search a doctor. In their eyes I'm afraid there's no such thing as a respectable Irishman."

After The Rising – April 1916

A stiffening breeze gusted along the street blowing sand and dust into Sean's face. He squinted his eyes and lowered his head. The breeze also carried the acrid smell of smoke – many of the city's buildings still smoldered.

Sean was anxious to be home and off the streets. He and his pistol had by now parted company. Already that day he had had two harrowing 'interviews' with British patrols. The British were taking no chances. Every Irish male civilian was for them a potential rebel in arms. People questioned in the street were left in no doubt as to the feelings of the soldiers. The interviews were hostile and the body searches humiliatingly thorough.

The people of the capital were now becoming increasingly aware of the government's hardening attitude. The good citizens still blamed the rebels of course. For the immediate future Dublin was a lonely place for Sean and his comrades. Sean walked the streets with all the paranoia of the hunted. Myles Flanaghan had proved correct in his cynical predictions of the British and Irish reactions to The Rising. The phenomena of house searches, though not as frequent as they would become, were already causing agitation amongst the populace. Trucks would suddenly screech to a halt. Then the clatter of steel shod boots, the doors battered in and the sudden violent influx of steel-helmeted, bayonet-wielding soldiers. Then the ensuing wreckage of a small home. A people unused to military occupation could never comprehend this awful violation of a person's most personal sanctuary. Hence the British with all the misplaced arrogance of a master race were unable to comprehend the awful immorality of their treatment of their Irish 'subjects'.

Sean nervously fumbled for his keys and opened his front door, to the very last second, expecting a voice challenging him. Once inside the eerie gloom of the apartment afforded a sense of escape – of sanctuary even. He lit the gas lamp and sat down on his bed, his back against the wall, his knees drawn up and his chin resting on his clasped hands. Sean stared fixedly at the damp, crumbling wall opposite. His mind raced over the events of the last two weeks – the shootings in Ashdeen, the deaths, the woundings, the burning buildings and the all pervading sense of danger. At first his feelings were of supercharged patriotism and bravery. Now he felt a strange fear and a cold cynicism that had hitherto been alien to him. He also felt a new sense of commitment. He knew it could not be over. Indeed it had only just begun. Did, as Flanaghan had always maintained, the apparent failure of the Rising, hide something different? A new beginning? A Rennaisance? Flanaghan's influence was in no small way responsible for his new visionary dedication. But would he stay the pace? What price would he personally have to pay?

Three short knocks on his door stirred him. He froze – suddenly apprehensive again. The knocks came again – low – secretive. Not the British surely? They would have arrived somewhat more flamboyantly – a rush, a charge, doors smashed, shouts and terror.

"Sean." A low soft voice – Andreena's. Sean's whole being surged with relief and sheer delight. He raced to the door and drew the locks. Andreena brushed in past him quickly, as though aware of his fear and his joy. She glowed with beauty. Her skin like porcelain, her blue, blue eyes sparkling. The fabulous red hair was neatly tied up under a blue beret, revealing the slender neckline. Her white blouse tucked firmly into the neat waistline of her blue skirt gave a wonderful fullness to her. Sean gazed as upon an angel.

She spoke softly, "Well Sean. A fine mess you're in. What'll you do?"

"Have you come to help or to scold?"

"Both I suppose. Though my fear is that you're beyond helping. Would I be right?"

She moved closer to him. It was the intimate closeness of a woman in love. Gently she ran a caressing finger through Sean's fore-lock.

"Beyond help? Not quite. I do need help right now. I need to get out of this city. I can't stand it here. Honest to God I'm like a prisoner in this chicken coop of a room. If I go out into the street I feel as though every pair of eyes was out to flay me alive. Oh no dear. I need to get away. My nerves won't take this much longer."

"I'll help you Sean. I'll get you away I promise. I'll bring you a change of clothes. Try to make you look less of a rebel. Spectacles and a walking cane. You'll look quite a gent. British soldiers are such snobs. They think only a poor man makes a rebel."

"Never thought you'd succumb to helping a rebel."

"I'm helping Sean Maloney. The man I love. Dam all causes, all love. To love you Sean."

"Very well," Sean whispered.

"And Sean – no more rows please. You come from what you come from and me from mine. Stay indoors until I come for you. We'll go to my uncle's. There's no one there but a few servants. You'll be safe enough."

They rushed into a spontaneous embrace. Andreena's kiss was warm and passionate. Within Sean a sudden blazing desire welled up. Andreena withdrew holding him at arm's length.

"Not now my love. Tomorrow I will come for you."

She turned quickly and hurried out. Sean listened as her footsteps retreated down the stairs and the front door opened and closed. He was alone again in the cold emptiness of the room.

Later that evening he went out. He ate at a cheap tea parlour in the city centre which, in spite of the shambles of the Rising, was still open for business as if by some divine work of providence. He even managed to buy a newspaper, its cover story all rage and invective against the rebels. Sean then made his way home down past the smouldering ruins of Sackville Street and then down the Quais. He stopped briefly on the City's famous Halfpenny Bridge and gazed back at the ravaged city.

'Had it all been worth it?' he thought. 'Surely it had to be.'

An innate pavlovian reflex made Sean freeze in fear. Off to his left a policeman was talking to a civilian. Paranoia or not, they were all too obviously talking about him. The civilian was pointing to Sean. British soldiers stood about them. They also looked Sean's way. How he had become the object of their attentions he did not know. Quickly he turned and hurried off the bridge. His pulse raced and so did his mind. He had to put distance between himself and the patrol. He felt he dared not run nor walk too fast – nothing to draw further suspicion nor invite a bullet in the back. He was being followed now – he was sure of it. Luckily the North Quay was crowded at that hour of the evening. He would lose himself in the throng. He moved quickly and quietly. A side street beckoned. His pace quickened now, almost to a run, but not quite. There could be no running yet. There might be another patrol just round the corner.

Fifteen minutes later and he was home again in the gloom of the apartment. He threw himself on the bed – panting, sweating profusely. The blood seemed to be pounding through his forehead.

'Who?' he thought, 'who I heaven's name could have recognized him? And who could possibly have wanted to turn him in?'

Faces rushed before him. The priest shouting in the roadway at Ashdeen. The publican. The face of the man talking to the peeler on the Quay. Where? Where had he seen that face before? The face was indeed familiar – the pale blue eyes, the long, drooping moustache and the red bloated cheeks. Then it hit him. The butcher. The butcher into whose shop he had escaped on the day of surrender.

"The treacherous, fuckin' scum!" Sean snarled aloud, "damn the bastard to hell!"

Andreena's visit had come none too soon. Now more than ever he had to leave the city.

For most of that night Sean did not sleep. When sleep did come it was the sleep of sheer exhaustion. Towards morning he began to wake – drowsily, stupidly – half in a dream. He heard trucks in the street and the door giving way. But it was a dream surely? The rush of heavy feet on the stairs and his own door crashing open – a dream surely? No. Rough hands seized him and hauled him from the bed. About him now he saw and heard the reality of the 'dream' – the English accents, the khaki uniforms and the Lee Enfields. A bright torch shone in his face dazzling him. He was thrown against the wall and pinioned.

"Let's get a look at him then," said an Irish accent.

"It's him alright."

In the dazzling light of the torch, Sean saw an R.I.C. man – peaked cap, toothbrush moustache, a hooked nose and a sneering smile of broken, crooked teeth.

"Well now. Thought you'd given us the slip eh? You sure are a slippery one. Well my lad all that's over – no more slipping about – not where you're going."

"Right lads take him out!"

May 1916

The river was in its spring flood. From under a willow Robbie observed its motion – not rippling, silent and flowing with a deep reassuring strength. The river was broad and grey – reflecting the overcast sky. Along the opposite bank ran a dusty road lined with a wattle fence. Tall swaying poplar trees grew along its length. Beyond the road gently sloping farmland. Insects buzzed in the warm spring afternoon's heat.

Beside Robbie, Dalton lay on his back, cap over his face, pulling on his braces with his thumbs. Robbie heard a rustling movement behind him.

"Fuck that French brew anyhow."

It was Hennessy, emerging from a thicket, fumbling with the buttons of his flies.

"Can't hold it! Eh Sean?" called Dalton.

"Well I've sure had enough. Let's walk some more lads. If I lie down now I'll never get up for a week."

"What's your hurry lad?"

"Fuck's sake lads!"

"Right! Right! We'll take a stroll", said Robbie. "Back to the village is good."

Lazily Robbie and Dalton got up. Carrying their tunics under their arms they made their way across a field to a narrow roadway. They walked an unhurried pace. Hennessy soon lagged behind – Robbie and Dalton walked on.

"Better put these tunics on. Might meet some officers."

"Hell no! Won't meet any officers here. Not posh enough for the bastards," said Robbie.

"Robbie you should have been an officer yourself. Your educated enough," said Dalton.

"No thanks. Bad enough being in the army at all."

" Why'd you join then?"

"Family pressure I suppose."

"Christ. Doesn't seem fair. I reckon a man shouldn't be here if he has no faith in it. My family were always in the army."

The cloud cover began to thin and the sunshine spread an all pervading glare over the landscape. Along the hedgerows butterflies fluttered among the wild flowers. Robbie plucked the head of wild poppy.

"These things seem to grow everywhere. Pretty. But they wither and die almost as soon as you pick them."

"Maybe you shouldn't pick them then? That cooing sound? What is it – a cuckoo?"said Dalton.

"Wood Pigeon," replied Robbie.

An oxen drawn farm cart lumbered into view. As it approached the friends got off the road and sat on the fence. The great beast moved with a solemn and majestic dignity. The cart, painted a bright red, creaked and trundled along behind. In the seat was an ageing farmer. He wore a blue cotton blouson and the inevitable black beret. His small, dark brown eyes twinkled in his lined and bronzed face. His clay pipe was clenched beneath a large drooping moustache. He smiled as he passed the three young Irishmen, baring his ancient blackened teeth.

"Bonjour mes enfants! Bonjour!" he called waving his bullock goad.

"Bonjour Monsieur!" the friends chorused in reply.

"Vive La France!" shouted Dalton.

"Vive l'Angleterre! Vive l'Angleterre!" came the reply.

The cart passed and the three friends jumped back onto the road. The stared after the cart for a minute then in silence turned and resumed their walk towards the village.

Suddenly Hennessy threw his tunic on the ground. He threw his hands skyward and yelled. "Fuck Angleterre! Fuck Angleterre! Vive Irlande! Vive Irlande!"

After an initial stunned silence his outburst caused Robbie and Dalton to erupt in fits of laughter. Dalton clutched at his sides and bent over from the waist and had to sit down on the roadway. Robbie laughed until his throat hurt. Tears ran down his face. Hennessy stood in the middle of the road his arms across his chest, obviously delighted with himself.

As suddenly as it started the laughter subsided. With the friends now in a distinctly light hearted mood, they resumed their stroll to the village. The thin veil of cloud had now dispersed, and the sun shone from a clear blue sky. The evening breeze was now warm and balmy and swayed the wild flowers on the roadside. Over by the river the tall Lombardy Poplars swayed majestically.

The friends donned their tunics on reaching the village. Making their way to the village square they found a small café.

June 1916

Robbie and his friends found themselves returning to the village quite often that summer. Whenever leave would allow the three friends found themselves making their way to the village. It seemed comfortably distant from the front. A medieval church was its focal point. Around this was the village square – the location for its weekly market .Just off the square was the small café that the friends had taken a 'shine' to. The tea drinking Irish were now acquiring a taste and a distinct preference for coffee – and of course the rich sweet smell of freshly baked French bread.

(Café, croissants et baguettes) the boys' knowledge of the essentials of the French language was definitely improving.

The small café held another attraction for Robbie. Her name was Jeanette. Very petite with wavy brown hair, hazel brown eyes and pearly white teeth that seemed to light up the room when she smiled. But she smiled seldom. A strange sadness seemed to haunt her.

Robbie soon found out why. She ran the café for her family. Her father and brothers were away at war. The French army had been locked in a desperate struggle with Germans at a place called Verdun. The casualty lists were enormous – the flower of French youth being lost in a maelstrom of shot, shell and now gas. War indeed was hell. Jeanette visited the town's ancient church every day. She prayed with other village women. Even the Curé, like most of the village men had gone off to war.

Jeanette had enough knowledge of English and with Robbie now a very keen student of 'le Francais' they were getting along really well – to Dalton and Hennessy's obvious delight. The teasing lasted all the way back to the front line. One late Sunday afternoon the friends were making their way back. The June evening was warm but an overcast sky beckoned rain. Dalton walked alongside Robbie. Hennessy was some paces behind , fumbling with his rolled up cigarette and sparking trench lighter.

Dalton broke the silence – no jesting this time.

"Ah yes Robbie she's a real diamond of girl. And don't deny it . You're smitten. Old cupid has shot his little arrows of at the pair of ye. But what d'you think? I mean the old religion thing?"

"Well I reckon I don't give a damn – not anymore. Surely if there's one thing this war emphasizes – we all send our dead to the same God. No agnostics in a trench."

"That's true Robbie."

"And that's not all. Coming over here to fight for God knows what. But you do see things differently. There's another world outside of our wee world. A world where people don't care if ye went to church on Sunday. Where people aren't concerned about the neighbour who owns the next ditch. And will they sell their cattle to him or hire him out at harvest time just on account of what church he goes to or doesn't go to."

"Yeah you're right Robbie. After a while none of it matters much."

A dull, rolling boom sounded from the horizon. The friends stopped . Each looked apprehensively to the horizon.

"S'okay," said Dalton, "it's not artillery – real thunder this time. Just look at them clouds. We'd best get a shift on."

Sudden heavy spits of rain lent an authority to his words.

"Rain damn it! And then the Kaiser's best friend! Mud! Damn bloody mud!"

Hennessy drew heavily on the remains of his cigarette.

"Can't be much. It is summer. Summer rain. Well that's the end of a good smoke."

July 1916

The rain had stopped – and so had the shelling. A strange silence had settled over the battlefield. The sky was clear and the warmth of the early morning sun was already baking the earth – the rising vapour could be seen across no-man's land – the German lines were a mirage-like shimmer.

In the British trenches the grim, ashen-faced men waited apprehensively. Few did not experience a tightening of the stomach muscles, nor grip their rifles so tightly that their knuckles glowed white. There was little talking apart from a few macabre jokes made to ease men's inward tension. There were those who still had not grasped the enormity of their great undertaking. For them this was but another trench raid for prisoners. All along the line men waited with resignation. The sun glinted on the fixed bayonets and the steel helmets – its heat was already causing discomfort.

The men all carried heavy packs of supplies. Some carried entrenching tools and barbed wire. What a cruel contradiction! Why carry such defensive items if they were expected to achieve a great sweeping break-through? Such was the tyranny of the trench warfare mentality and the intellectual bankruptcy of the military mind. A naïve belief persisted amongst all ranks, that the intense bombardment of the previous five days would have effectively suppressed all opposition. Sceptics were few – one of them was Robert McBride.

"Let's hope the bombardment's done its work," said Robert.

"Course it has," replied Dalton, raising his helmet and wiping the sweat from his brow, "nothing could have survived that surely to Christ. And even so – anything that did wouldn't be fit to fight. I just wish we'd get going."

"Don't know," said Robert, "suppose the hun's been expectin' us. Suppose he quit his forward trenches when the barrage started and then has rushed back now it's over. Been sittin' waitin' on us."

"Not so. The hun's good but not that good," another soldier interjected. His drawn nervous face belied his confident words.

A series of shrill whistle blasts sounded all along the line. Like a rippling movement on water, the lines of men began to move. Pushing and jostling as in a bus queue, the khaki clad figures scrambled out of their trenches and began moving toward the German lines. The advancing troops presented a curious air of orderliness and calm. Yet out in the open, away from the safety of the dugout, many felt especially vulnerable. Nobody hurried. All moved forward at a steady pace, with their bayonets fixed, straining under their heavy packs. Lewis guns were casually carried shoulder high.

Robert looked around him – at the still quiet German lines and behind him, to his left and right, at his own line from where, ever increasing numbers of men were spilling out onto the wasted ground of no-man's land, like a swarm of ants leaving a crack in a pavement.

Again Robert looked before him to the German lines. Inside his tunic his body sweltered in the July heat. His mouth was parched. The sweat from his brow stung his eyes. He squinted as he gazed forward. A dancing silver haze shimmered over the German line. Then the awful realization dawned on him. The German wire was still intact. Five days of bombardment and the wire was still largely intact. His mind raced with questions. Would they get through? Had enough gaps been blasted? Would there be any opposition.

His answers came swiftly and brutally. The air suddenly filled with the high pitched whines of German shells. Explosion followed explosion. Screams pierced the air. More shells raced through the air, screeching, wailing like a thousand banshees, exploding in a crescendo of ear-splitting bangs.

The British now surged forward – no longer in steady strides. Now all was a desperate sprint – on – on to the German wire. Robert looked about him. Mick Dalton was still with him, as was Sean Hennessy and Willie Scott. Then through the shells and the yells could be heard another sound – a deadly, furious, incessant rattle. A rattle with an all too familiar rhythm of death – death in all its terrible finality – machine guns.

All round Robert men were being hit. Men screamed, threw their arms skyward, leapt into the air, convulsed and writhed as they fell. Others merely stopped in their tracks, hung suspended on the air by their last life force, then slowly, graciously, crumpled to the ground.

Wounded, mutilated men were already lying on the ground screaming – out of their minds in agony.

Still the British moved forward. Nearer and nearer came the German lines. Robert felt the earth shake at his feet as it was spattered with machine-gun fire. Then Hennessey was hit. He issued a blood-curdling scream. He dropped his rifle. His body frozen, contorted, impaled on the air. His face and chest were a bloodied mess. Then he collapsed and was still.

Willie Scott went down, rolling onto his back, and bringing his shattered knees up to is chest, clasping his shins. His face twisted in agony. From behind him, a soldier grabbed the shoulder strap of Scott's pack and attempted to drag him forward to the cover of a shell crater. Again the gunners found their mark. The rescuer screamed, spun and pirouetted before falling. Scott's legs bolted straight out. His arms collapsed by his sides. The back-pack made his body arch gracefully, head back, neck outstretched, mouth agape, eyes wide and suddenly still.

Closer and closer yet to the German lines. Through the white veil of gun smoke Robert could see the steel helmets of the defenders, He could see the machine guns also, belching death and voraciously feeding from the ammunition belts. Like winnowing hooks in a cornfield they mercilessly thinned the British ranks.

Robert saw Dalton dive for cover behind a corpse and begin to snipe at the German lines. Robert followed suit. Quickly he undid his pack, letting it fall before him. He also went to ground. Using the scant protection of his pack he aimed his rifle. His target was a machine gunner barely twenty yards off to his right. Robert squeezed the trigger, felt his rifle kick and saw his target, arms thrown aloft, go reeling back into the bottom of the trench. The gunner's mate reacted quickly, grasping the gun and swinging it to bear in their direction. The two men hugged the earth as bullets spattered and ricocheted about them. The corpse in front of Dalton shook convulsively under the impact. The hail of fire moved away and Dalton seized his chance. The gunner's mate was hit in the face, the bridge of his nose being carried away. His face suddenly a bloodied mask the German followed his comrade to the bottom of the trench.

From behind more waves of British infantry were pressing forward. Three men by-passed Robert and Dalton only to have to dive for cover as a grenade was lobbed from the German trench. One man was not quick enough going to ground. He took the full force of the blast and was flung back onto the barbed wire. He did not even scream. The flesh had been seared from his now skull-like face. His body hung suspended on the wire, arms outstretched like a macabre scarecrow.

A sergeant came up from behind. He carried a Lewis gun. There was a wild possessed look in his eye. More troops followed on his heels.

"On your feet! On your feet! Forward! You'll buy it for sure if ya stay here! Forward!"

The sergeant aimed bursts of fire at the German trenches. Dalton was on his feet now. Robert rose also. The effort to get off the ground was terrifying given the basic animal instinct to hug the earth. But once up Robert was sprinting forward. The Irish were at last carrying the German line. The defenders either fell back or were killed. Few surrendered.

At last, Robert's party gained the German trenches. Robert leapt across the first one.

"Grenades!" yelled the wild eyed sergeant, "Use grenades on the dugouts! Then get going."

The grenades detonated with dull muffled thuds beneath them. A shot rang out close by. A soldier beside Robert screamed and fell back into the trench. Robert spun about to confront a wild eyed German youth holding a pistol in the meager cover of a shallow shell-crater. Robert fired from the hip. The German boy fell back then scrambled to his feet again. He attempted to raise his pistol again. He never did. Robert used his bayonet. Leaping into the crater he plunged the steel into the boy's stomach. Robert felt the terrible, sickening sensation as his steel penetrated the boy's flesh. The German's body froze as he clutched vainly at Robert's rifle – his face contorted and bewildered, his glassy blue eyes now strangely peaceful.

Robert was filled with a sickening horror at himself. He did not get long to indulge the feeling. The battle, as relentless as ever, intervened. The earth shook as a great crescendo of German shells exploded about them. Instinctively the men went to ground. Robert sheltered in the same crater as the German boy he had just killed. When the respite came the sergeant's voice was again to be hard yelling insanely in the din.

"C'mon! C'mon! On your feet! On your feet! Let's move! Move!"

Robert, now eager to leave the dead behind, needed less urging this time. He scrambled out of the crater. They had barely covered twenty yards when the German barrage came screaming down again. Robert felt the sudden sensation of pain and saw the sergeant's petrified body silhouetted in an orange flash. As he fell, Robert saw two lifeless crows dangling on the barbed wire. The sky became a golden cornfield dancing beneath a blazing yellow sun. Then, mercifully – oblivion.

★ ★ ★

Robert tried to open his eyes, but the sensation of light, and the pain in his head were too much for him. He was aware of numbness in his legs. His whole body ached. He was lying on his back with his head propped up on a knapsack. Moving his right hand to his face he felt the dry, caked blood on his cheek. Moving his fumbling fingers further he felt the bandage.

"A head wound," he mumbled. His mind now raced with questions – fearful, hopeful, "How bad? Not that bad surely? I suppose I got off light. Hell Robbie lad – you got off light surely. You're still alive, That's better then many a poor bastard."

At last Robbie forced his eyes open. He tried to rise, forcing himself up on his elbows. He lay where he had fallen. The earth felt warm beneath. The smell of smoke hung on the air, then he saw his legs. Both were bandaged – the left in splints.

"Oh shit! Oh Jesus Christ!"

Robbie felt something metallic inside his tunic. Putting his hand to his chest he found a whiskey flask.

"Dalton'. Well good for you old pal. Here's hoping you made it."

He pulled the stopper and drank. Swallowing hard he lay back gasping.

"Alright Irish take it easy me old mate," an English accent called. The man approached and knelt down. "You'll be alright mate." Robbie recognized the Red Cross armbands.

"You bind me up?"

"Yeah, I did. Sorry I had to leave you. But I got a lot of other blokes to see. You'll be moved as soon as a stretcher becomes available."

"What sort of shape am I in then?"

"Oh hell son! You're not so bad. Shrapnel wounds. One to the head's just a crease – no penetration. Too soon to say about your legs. But I seen a helluva lot worse. Hell lad. This is your ticket back to good old Blighty – or should I say Belfast. Well I've to move on. We'll move you just as soon as we've a stretcher free."

The man moved off and Robbie gulped more whiskey. He thought of Dalton and hoped he was still alive. He thought of Brayspont, his farm and his family. He thought of Jeanette.

"You'll be alright lad." The orderly's words kept ringing in his ears. His head hurt. For a so called crease it really hurt. A wooden stake was close by. Close enough for his to move over to it and prop his back against it. He had a better view of his surroundings now. The sun was now low in the sky behind the British lines. It was late evening. Robbie realised he had been unconscious all day. The battle had moved further east as the intermittent sounds of the guns now attested to. From the nearby German trench he heard English voices. Not the English of the orderly. It was the English of a public school – a strange affected tongue that was as alien to him as to the orderly. It was the affected tongue of the master class – one's supposed social betters. The talk was from those who knew what was best for the world. These were the architects of disaster. They were now inspecting the hard won German trenches and expressing amazement at their depth and at the industry of their opponents.

The earth around Robbie was dry and warm from the day's sunshine. In parts it was scorched black from the shelling. Close by a working party was still cutting away the

German wire. Away to his left a man was trying to cut a body free. Far out into no-man's land, stretcher parties were moving the dead and dying to the rear. Death was everywhere. Bodies lay sprawled obscenely on the ground or pathetically festooning the barbed wire. The warm evening air smelled of gun smoke and dead flesh. The flies buzzed incessantly.

"Imagine that," came a voice from the dugout, "got to be at least forty feet deep. Well I'll say!"

From the British trenches a line of infantry was moving forward. The column moved like a strange khaki centipede across the pitted lunar landscape, snaking its way round the shell craters. To Robbie their faces all seemed blank, no eyes, no noses – featureless. There was no talking in the ranks. The centipede moved noiselessly, as in some aquarium like world. Closer. They passed over the newly won German trenches. Closer. They marched passed Robbie. Taking little notice of him. The few men who looked his way merely stared blankly at someone who was now just another remnant of the day's carnage, littering the battlefield. Robbie perceived their gaunt, hungry looks – each man apprehensive for his own chances in the fight ahead.

"Replacements! Poor bastards!" A dry rasping voice sounded behind him.

"C'mon. Let's get this one."

At last, a stretcher party. Laying the stretcher alongside him the medics gently placed Robert on it. The men did not speak. Their faces were grim and weary – their eyes blank and expressionless. Slowly, steadily, they set off across no-man's land to the British rear, and the safe sterile world of a field dressing station.

Then the roaring, whining sound of German shells filled the air. The orderlies froze in a pavlovian reflex of fear. Yet they did not go to ground. For the men judged that the shells would pass them by and explode well into the British rear. Being attuned to the sound of the shells was something which was soon acquired by men whose every nerve sought survival. The men moved forward again – slowly faltering every few yards on the rough ground. The shells exploded, indeed well into the British rear. The bombardment lasted several minutes. The orderlies continued stoically onward. A minute later – more shells. This time the British reply screaming towards the Germans – death making its return journey. As suddenly as it had started the barrage stopped. Only the rattle of small arms fire in the distance and the crump of the trench mortars punctuated the evening air. From the nearness of the sounds Robert reckoned that the enemy had not been pushed back very far. There had been no big breakthrough. There was to be no respite from the carnage.

"So much for the big push," muttered Robert and he reached again for Dalton's flask, "and all for what?"

Yet Robert felt that somehow he had made it. He had been through the maelstrom and survived. He had a sense of being saved. He lay on his back looking upward at the darkening sky, conscious only of the movement of the stretcher. He felt he was in the care of the Supreme Being, and that these orderlies were his guardian angels, spiriting him away across the bloodied, tortured earth – away from their Dantean inferno.

The orderlies left Robbie on a field ambulance which would take him the rest of the way to a dressing station. Without speaking the men set off again, with their stretcher, back to the smoke and the sounds of battle. Robbie watched them go, trudging with a wearied, resigned air. In the west the sun was setting, casting its red glow over the bloodied, smoldering earth.

Someone in the ambulance was crying – a low pathetic, whimpering sound.

"The poor bastard thinks he gonna be blind," said a soldier who squatted on the floor, nursing a wounded arm. Robert turned to see a small, stockily built man, with keen blue eyes and red hair. He had a flat boxer's nose and big ears, all the more accentuated by his close-cropped military haircut.

"Where you from lad?" asked the small soldier.

"Brayspont."

"Brayspont. One nice wee place. I've often been. Gone down on the train with mi Ma and Da. Ain't been since I was a wee lad. From Belfast myself. So – a Belfast man and a Brayspont man stuck in the middle of all this. What are we doing here? Fighting somebody else's war. Y'know. Our boys advanced the farthest distance today. An' what happens? We run straight into our own fuckin' barrage! Our own fuckin' barrage! Didn't expect us to advance so quickly. So they say."

"Hell!" came another voice, "they meant it alright. They knew what they were doin'. Slaughter the Ulsterman so there's nobody left to stop Home Rule."

The trauma had accentuated the Ulsterman's inherent paranoia.

"Stupid fuckin' officers! Couldn't plan a piss up in a brewery."

"Better try and stop this lad crying so much. He'll give us

all the fuckin' creeps," said the small Belfast man. He then moved to the back of the ambulance.

"Alright lad – alright. Here have a cigarette. Mightn't be that bad at all."

The slender waif of a soldier sat hunched in the rear corner of the ambulance. His young frame seemed frozen with fear. His face was completely bandaged above the nose. His sparse fair hair was knotted with sweat and blood. The small Belfast man crammed the cigarette into one corner of his mouth and lit up. After a few draws the boy started to gag. The Belfast man withdrew the butt.

"Easy lad, easy."

The ambulance engine started up and with a lurching, bumping movement it pulled away toward the rear. The sudden movement made the Belfast soldier grimace in pain.

"C'mon lad," he continued to the sobbing wreck in front of him, "don't let them officers hear you cry. Chin up."

"Fuck the officers. Stupid bastards!" somebody hissed.

"Y'know," said another, "I charged across that no-man's land with mi rifle, bayonet fixed. Bloody great pack on mi back. Got myself shot. And a never killed one single German. Not one I tell you."

"Well lucky you. You got a clear conscience," said the Belfast man, "who wants to kill a German anyhow. They done nothing on us."

"Too right. Every last one of them is some mother's son."

"Thanks be to fuck we're getting out of it."

Eventually the ambulance came to a halt. They seemed to have been traveling for some time. Robert noticed that the quality of the road had improved shortly before they stopped

– less bumps and jerks. The tailboard slammed down and the walking wounded got out first. After climbing down the Belfast soldier collapsed.

"He's alright. Wound's opened up though. He's lost a lot of blood," said a distinctly feminine voice.

"He has indeed. His clothes are soaking poor lad," said another distinctly feminine voice, "quickly sergeant."

A few minutes later Robbie's stretcher was lifted. He was carried to a tent. The field hospital was laid out in rows of tents. Each tent's window was covered with a mosquito net. From inside, paraffin lamps burned with a white glow. The summer night was warm and the air was heavy with the smell of ether and paraffin. Robbie drank the remainder of Dalton's whiskey in the ambulance. His mind was confused again. He thought of home. He thought of Scott and Hennessey. Then he saw a broad river lined with poplar trees. Scott and Hennessey were on the other side. He could not hear them. They waved their caps in a gesture of farewell. A French girl was bathing in the river. On his temple he could feel someone's fingers, cool and gentle. He heard the cutting sound of scissors, slow, deliberate. His bandages were being changed. There were no battle sounds. No acrid stench of smoke. Only the hissing of the paraffin lamps and the clinical, incandescence of its mantle. And the scissors moving and the cool caressing touch of the fingers. At the river bank the French girl stood up out of the water.

November 1916

he air was crisp and clear, the sort of bright autumn day Robert loved. He felt glad to be alive. Glad to be back in Ireland after his ordeal in France. He limped slowly along the canal bank, throwing his weight on his sturdy walking cane. The day before had been his first back in Ireland and today his first back in its augustan capital. The destruction wrought by the rising had dismayed but not shocked him. Dublin for him was as ever beautiful. Indeed in all this city's moods and aspects it was to Robert magnificent.

Robert was in a reflective mood that morning. He had much to reflect on – France, Brayspont, his farm, The Rising and Dublin on this clear, cold November morning. He thought of Andreena. He now knew of her affair with Sean Maloney. He knew also why it had ended. He felt a certain sadness, for he had always liked Sean in spite of his diehard republicanism. Sean, he knew, was, or at least should have been his enemy. Yet he could never bring himself to dislike him.

His reverie was disturbed by a commotion further up the road. Near a footbridge, a group of people were gathered at the canal bank. Clearly their focus of attention was something in the canal. As he drew nearer Robert realised that the something was, or had been, someone. A body was being dragged from the water. An accident? A suicide? Surely not a murder? Drawing closer Robert saw the deathly pale face, the stiff limbs, the long black dress – a young woman. A blanket was produced and her petrified form covered. Two policemen then lifted her further up the bank. Two soldiers watched impassively. Some old Dublin women dressed in black, clutched their rosary beads and drew their shawls more closely about them. One old lady began to cry. Some nuns arrived and knelt near the body. Robert now stood next to the group. The body was indeed quite lifeless. On the ground about her, canal water from her clothes had melted the morning frost and had frozen again.

Robert stood for a minute, transfixed by this pitiable sight. The old woman whimpered. The nuns' murmured prayers.

"Must have been in the water all night, poor soul."

"What could have driven her to it?"

"Sure she couldn't have known what she was doing."

"Who was she?" Robert asked an elderly man who stood silently in the cold. The old man turned and looked at Robert. His eyes were grey and misty and sunk into a gaunt unshaven face. He drew slowly on his clay pipe and spoke.

"A wee lassie from de nort'. Came down here with her husband, Lord rest him. He was killed in the rising. Poor fella – he was a nortener too. An' that very day didn't she have her child. Stillborn. I ask you. Sure isn't it small wonder she ended up like this. Must have been out of her mind poor soul."

Robert moved on. He was aware of an innate fascination with the dead. He could do no good. Decency he felt demanded that he move on. As he left a priest arrived, out of breath and draping a stole around his neck.

"A priest! Let the priest through."

"The last rites God bless her."

"Sure maybe her soul hasn't left her body yet."

From behind him Robert could hear voices, raised in a steady rhythmic chant. The Catholic Rosary was being said.

Belfast Lough, Spring 1917

The waters of the lough were still – grey like the sky above. The fishing boat drifted quietly on the current. Behind it followed an aerial chorus of terns and gulls – wheeling, arcing then suddenly stopping, hanging imperceptible in the afternoon's soft, misty light, then plummeting downward into the boat's wake.

Drifting on the current may have seemed pointless to the unwary onlooker. This boat drifted with a purpose. From beneath his black peaked cap the keen eyes of her skipper constantly searched the seascape before him. A small, bearded fisherman in his forties, he set his arm on the tiller. Clad in a thick wool coat and waterproof leggings, a pipe was stuck jauntily between his stained broken teeth. Then he saw what he wanted. Looming, dark and eerie out of the mist, the squat ugly shape of the prison ship.

"Mister Muller! Mister Muller!" called the helmsman.

From beneath a tarpaulin a dark figure emerged onto the deck. Young and of athletic build the man's closely cropped blond hair showed beneath his navy cap. He wore a dark navy double breasted tunic over dark wool trousers and navy boots.

"Well there she is Mister Muller. His Majesty's Prison

141

ship. Crammed to the gills wi' good Irish rebels. Take yi good note of her mind."

"Do not worry Mister Flynn. If she goes down, I assure you fe jairmanz fill not be responsible. How soon to land?"

"'Bout twenty minutes now sir. Best you stay below from here on sir. Getting' damn close to the sentries."

★ ★ ★

"Shit! Bloody British shit! That's what it is!"

"It's sure not for eatin'."

"Sunday! The one day in the week we get meat and look! The beef's like leather, the spuds are slush an' the cabbage isn't even cooked. I think the bastards are trying to kill us off slowly," Sean looked despondently at the dish in front of him.

"Well I'm not even gonna even try to eat the bloody shit," said Reilly, who then rose from the edge of his bunk and moved toward the port hole of the cabin that served as their prison cell. He looked out across the still, grey waters of the lough toward the County Down coastline.

"There's a fog movin' in from the seaward," said Reilly, "sure gives me the creeps."

"Fog's no harm," said Sean, "ain't nothin' out there but water and fish."

"What if something bigger than this, rams us in the fog?"

"This is the biggest thing you'll get on this lough. Next biggest is a fishin' smack. Look Reilly – we'll not be here forever. Try not to torment yourself."

"I don't know. You always are the optimist Sean. But I keep thinking we've had it. Do you know what I bin thinking?

Suppose a German u-boat torpedoes this thing. It's a real possibility. How are the Germans to know this is a prison ship? And suppose the British decide to mine her – blame it on a German torpedo. Be rid of us right an' handy then. That'd be just up their street – the devious bastards. Perfidious Albion I tell you."

"In the name of Jasus Reilly you're a real cheer. Such a prophet of doom I never knew. What in the name o'Christ did I do to get locked up with a morbid ballocks like you? Now come an' eat your food."

"That shit?"

"Look! If you don't eat it you'll die. You'll die if you worry and you'll die if you don't worry – never mind fucking torpedoes and mines."

"Fuck it! I suppose you're right Sean. That's another irritating habit of yours Sean. You're always fucking right."

Sean laughed. Reilly came back to the edge of his bunk and began to eat. Half an hour later the cell door opened. It was exercise time. Sean was joined on deck by Flanaghan.

"God knows how long this'll go on Sean. But the British'll not keep us locked up forever. An' if they think it's finished they'll have to execute a lot more than just seven of us."

"Yes Myles. But what of Germany? Things aren't looking so good for her."

"True. The Americans have joined the war on Britain's side. You know Sean I never did have much faith in the Americans. How naïve so many are looking for salvation from that quarter. Small nations are just small nations I'm afraid. Their helping the British will certainly tilt the balance. But we don't now what the new Russian Government will do. A separate peace there will free more soldiers to face the British and the French. But all this should be meaningless to us. German victory, German defeat – Ireland's struggle for freedom goes on. If we should fail – our failure will only lend strength to another generation of rebels."

By now Sean had this distinct feeling that Flanaghan needed a platform. For the speech was not for him. Flanaghan now had the look of a man caged. He moved to the edge of the deck and stood grasping the rail that was the wall for the prisoner's 'exercise yard'. Flanaghan stared at the County Down coastline now shrouded in a fog bank. Tiny droplets of mist formed on the lenses of his spectacles. The afternoon air was cold and Flanaghan shivered under his great coat. His steely eyes were set firmly toward the coast.

January 1923

Sean and his company were hiding out on a small deserted farm in the mountains to the south of Newquay. The mountains were barren in mid winter – gorse naked of bloom, ferns a lifeless brown and the upper mountain slopes thinly covered with snow.

Sean had taken the small cottage for his quarters. The rest of the section had converted the out houses into sleeping quarters. Bales of hay served as mattresses. Empty oil drums had been converted into stoves. The previous occupant had left a good supply of cut dried turf – this and dry rotten timber served as a fuel supply.

The farm buildings were clustered in a small sheltered valley. Sentries were posted on the tops of the nearby hills. Pat Dolahan was posted on top of what was probably the most important hill – that which overlooked the narrow loanan which came from the southern and only approach to the farm.

It was late afternoon and the sun was setting low in the western sky. Parts of the loanan were illumined by the brilliant sunshine, other parts were cast in shadow by the hills.

Pat found sentry duty boring. But today he was more alert than usual. He had been told to expect a contact from Dublin. Suddenly in the evening sunshine a figure appeared. Pat had difficulty seeing him at first in the glare. Then the newcomer moved into the shade. In the half light Pat could see a tall, broad-shouldered figure, clad in a navy blue greatcoat. A grey cloth cap was pulled over a mass of flaming red hair. Over one shoulder he carried a bag. The stranger walked at a brisk pace.

Pat turned and whistled down toward the camp – three shrill cries imitating a curlew. When he turned again the stranger had stopped and was looking around him suspiciously. The curlew cries had not fooled him. He resumed his onward pace. As he drew level with Pat's position, Pat sprang from cover.

"Hold it! Stand right there!"

The newcomer stopped and found himself looking down the barrel of a mauser. Pat's stance was firm, determined.

"Who are you?" asked the stranger.

"Well now. I'm sure as hell not the yeoman o' the guard. And I'll ask the questions. Now! Who are you?"

"It's alright Pat," called another voice, "this is Captain Plunkett."

From the bushes behind Pat strode another rebel Jack Magee. Jack had obviously come in response to the curlew call and was not, quite out of breath. Jack curtly saluted. Eamonn Plunkett came sharply to attention and returned the salute. Then spontaneously, Eamonn and Jack shook hands.

"From our Dublin command," continued Jack to Pat, "and I believe a native of these parts."

"That's right," said Eamonn, "a Brayspont man, born and bred."

"Doubt if you'll get a chance to visit home. The town's hiving with Tans. Newquay is even worse. If your face is on a wanted poster, its not advisable."

"How's your glorious leader?"

Jack evaded the question at first.

"Okay Pat. I'll take the Captain on in. Someone will relieve you in an hour."

Dolahan tipped his cap in acknowledgement and retreated back to the cover of the hedgerow. After walking some distance to the camp Jack finally answered.

"Our glorious leader as you call him, is not so well I'm afraid. Captain Maloney has been drinking. I'd tread softly sir."

"Why?"

"He scares me sometimes. Gets into this deep depression. Becomes, moody and unpredictable. He's very much a changed man from when you knew him.

"Tread softly." Magee's caution was still in Eamonn's ears as he opened the door of the cottage. Inside the air smelled of turf smoke and whiskey. The room was low ceilinged. Between the rafters the bare thatch of the roof was visible. In the open hearth a low turf fire burned. Opposite was a bunk, a small table and chair. On the table a kerosene lamp burned its mantle bright and hissing. At the right of the hearth was an oaken welsh dresser, stacked with willow patterned crockery – no doubt the previous occupant's pride.

"Well – well – well! Our illustrious Captain Plunkett!"

Sean stood in the kitchen doorway. Unshaven, his face lined and drawn, his eyes were staring, their pupils dilated with drink.

"Sean! You're drunk!"

"Really now! Oh don't be cross. A man has to relax. Find some sort of spiritual release. Sit down Eamonn. Sit down."

Sean gestured toward a stool by the hearth. Uneasily, Eamonn sat down. Sean sat in a rocking chair, resting his feet on the edge of the bunk.

"Well what can you expect. Here I am. Holed up on this piss arse of a mountain. What do you expect?"

"Your men aren't drunk. I'm not drunk. We've all to live through this."

"Yes. We've all to live through this and somehow remain a human being. What have you come here for? To lecture on morality? Sobriety?"

"I've come with new orders for you."

"To hell with orders. To hell with all of it. You see Eamonn I've had it. I go to sleep at night and wake up hearing screams in my head."

Sean put his hands to his head and frowned deeply, shutting his eyes tightly. Suddenly Sean sat bolt upright in his chair and drew his pistol! His eyes were open – staring wildly. His mind in a whirl. He trembled all over. Eamonn froze – sensing imminent danger. Then just as suddenly Sean relaxed. He stared at his pistol with a sad fascination.

"This has been a cold mistress. Cold, cold, cold and dreadful. There's been too much killing. I don't really know if I can go on with it. All for what? Ireland? D'you think Ireland'll thank us. Sure. When we're all dead an' gone or failing old men, they'll sing wonderful songs about us. But what of us? Now? Next month? Next year if this awful fucking thing ends? Who'll want men like us?"

Sean raised his pistol, squinted down the sight and fired. A plate on the dresser shattered. He fired again. Crockery shards scattered about the room. Eamonn remained frozen on his stool, wincing in fright. Another shot! A splinter struck Eamonn's cheek. Eamonn leapt to his feet.

"Damn you Sean! Control yourself!"

"Get out," Sean hissed, "go on get out!"

Eamonn, now sensing his mortal peril, looked for the door. Without turning his back, he retreated. All the way the two men eyed each other coldly. On gaining the door, Eamonn turned sharply and hurried outside. More shots rang out.

"What the hell is it?" called Magee.

"Oh just a little target practice. I suppose he'll just have to sleep it off if he doesn't kill himself in the meantime. Does he have many of these bouts o'drinking?"

"Lately – yes. Too many I'm afraid. I expect he'll do his Lady Macbeth act in the morning."

"Lady Macbeth act?"

"Washes himself. Over and over again. Just isn't healthy."

That night Eamonn shared supper with the rest of the men in the outhouses. There was a singing session later. But the atmosphere remained tense.

★ ★ ★

The trap raced along the road out of Brayspont to Rosseena. The pony trotted at a steady pace. Striding majestically over the pitted muddy surface his hooves beat a regular rhythm to the grinding of the trap's wheels. The trap's driver was Fred Gant. Fred looked unusually dignified as he sat bolt upright in the driver's seat. His advancing years were mellowing his infamous 'wicked' temperament and the frequency of his drinking bouts.

His passenger, sitting demurely by his side, was Mai Casey. Mai clutched her long wool shawl closely against the fresh April breeze. The countryside raced by as the road took the pair past the rippling waters of the lough. At the roadside the tall sycamores swayed in the wind, shaking from their new leaves droplets of rain water. All about them nature's miracle of spring was unfolding. The countryside was greener and held an air of freshness and renewal.

They moved away from the loughside and drove past Brayspont cemetery. Mai started as she noticed a lone figure near a recently dug grave. Her pulse quickened. A young man in a trench coat, there was something clearly familiar about him. At once she felt fear and a sense of longing. The trap had sped well beyond the cemetery when Mai frantically called on Fred to stop.

"Wha! Whoa!" Fred growled at the pony as he drew rein.

"What in heaven's name ails ya chile? What's the matter?"

"Never mind now Fred. Just let me down."

"But whatever for? In the middle of a country road and this far from town?"

"Look I – oh Fred I'll see you again. Keep an eye out for me on the way home. I just have to be on my own right now. I'll see you."

"Oh well. Mine's not to reason why I suppose," said the bewildered Fred. Then turning to the pony he flicked the reins over her back and goaded her on.

"C'mon g'yup there! G'yup!"

Mai skipped over the puddles as she ran. The hems of her wool skirt were splattered with mud when she reached the cemetery. The old gate creaked wearily as she entered and then clanged shut behind her. Instinctively she made for the graves of Dermot and Mary Maloney.

There was as yet no headstone. But the floral wreaths were still fresh, unravaged by the elements. Mai could at first see no one. She suddenly seemed alone in the quiet of the graveyard. The only sounds were the wind gently rushing through the trees and Mai's own breathing. Out of breath, little droplets of sweat made her complexion tingle and glow. Her cheeks flushed radiantly.

"Mai."

She turned quickly to see Sean Maloney emerge from between the sycamores.

"Sean!" Mai called his name in disbelief, smiling. "Why were you hiding on me Sean?"

"Well now Mai I wasn't to know it was you, was I? I mean I have to be careful these days. You made enough noise to wake the dead. Suppose I should not be so irreverent."

Sean looked longingly at her as he spoke. Yet his eyes held a deep sadness. Mai's face now lost its smile. She trembled. Her voice sounded troubled and urgent.

"Oh Sean. What good'll this do? I know you are mourning but you can't stay. They'll get you as well. Too many know you about here. The town's full of Tans. First your parents, now you too."

"No I don't think so Mai. Not yet. I've too much to do."

"You mean scores to settle. That's what you're really saying isn't it Sean. But where's all this leading to. This never ending spiral of passion and hate. It's destroying you Sean. First that McBride girl."

"You mean Andreena. Mai that's long since past. A wound that's healed. I've no regrets of bitterness over that."

Sean spoke without conviction. Avoiding Mai's eyes and gazing seaward as he spoke.

"And this? Hasn't this made you bitter. Your own parents

murdered? Of course who can blame you? But will it do any good?" Mai was pleading now, her voice close to breaking.

"Oh Mai! I do so need you now. Help me!"

They rushed into a passionate spontaneous embrace. Mai's lips were warm and full with passion. Her cheeks wet against his. Then Sean drew back slightly.

"Mai. Hide me. For just a few days."

"Sean you're crazy. Get away now before its all too late."

"Oh God in heaven I can't. I just have to stay – for a few days at least. But then I'll go. I promise."

Mai's eyes reached into his. She knew that he would be hers for a very short time. Her hand gently stroked his cheek, then wistfully she trailed her fingers through his hair.

"Sean of course I'll hide you. God help us, will we never know peace again. Sean you're a fool. You're doomed and I can feel it."

"Yes Mai I know." Sean's voice trailed into a tender whisper, "we're caught up by force greater than we can understand. We're being carried along in the current, headin' for the rapids, and I don't even wanna try getting' to the bank."

Spring 1923

The mountains around Newquay were thickly gorse covered. Some areas had been recovered for pasturing sheep. Most of the flocks grazed on the lower slopes. Gorse and hawthorn prevailed on the rocky lower slopes.

Sean and his company hid along a ditch fronted by a stone wall. Their position overlooked a railway line. Beyond a turn in the line, obscured by a rocky hilltop, was a small railway halt – the company's objective that day.

Myles Flanaghan sat halfway up the slope, looking towards the bend in the line – the familiar cigarette holder clenched in his teeth. He stirred at the approach of Sean Maloney and another young rebel. They walked quite openly up the track – no fear of being seen.

"Just the guard in his control box. No passengers on the platform ,"Sean reported.

"Good. We'll move quickly."

The small band left the protection of their stone walled ditch and moved in the direction of the railway halt. The plan was to ambush an incoming government train. The control office was quickly occupied. The elderly guard was allowed to walk away in the direction of the nearest village. No one even considered the possibility of his raising the alarm, given the distance to the village and the lack of phones in rural Ireland in those days.

An engine lay in a siding. This was got under steam. Diverting this into the path of the incoming government troop train would now be the main element of the rebel plan. Most of the group positioned themselves on the high ground above the line. Sean, Flanaghan and small group occupied the guard's control box. A shrill whistle blast from the south announced the imminent arrival of the troop train.

"Courteous of them to announce their arrival," Flanaghan sneered with all the menace of a striking cobra.

"These levers diverting the train – have you moved them?"

"Yes. Already done," replied Sean.

" Tell our boys in that engine, to move as soon as the 'staters' round the bend. The minute they're in view start rolling."

The government train rounded the bend whistling as she did so. The engine pushed an open sandbagged wagon before it – this mounted a heavy machine gun. Two more wagons were pulled behind, each carrying troops in the uniform of the newly-formed Free State army.

The rebel plan worked like clockwork. The rebel-manned engine moved quickly out of its siding and onto the main line – heading directly for the incoming train. The rebel 'crew' jumped clear. An immediate panic gripped the government train. Brakes screeched as the whistle sounded frantically. Men started jumping for their lives. When it came the crash was tremendous The searing , grinding, crashing of steel pierced the ears. The trains derailed and wagons overturned. When the tumult subsided only the hissing of steam and the groans of the injured could be heard. Then the rebel position erupted in a fusillade of shots and then just as suddenly – silence.

The rebels peered down on the carnage – fascinated. Then slowly they left the shelter of their position and made their way down to the line – to survey their handiwork.

The rebels moved cautiously amongst the dead. None moved. All were still. Both engines, like the wagons, lay on their sides – some wheels still spinning, one engine continuing to emit regular belches of steam. Flynn climbed atop the government machine and peered in curiously. A single shot rang out. The rebels, to a man , froze. Nerves were suddenly taut. Knuckles glowed white. Then Flynn atop the engine dropped his rifle with a clatter and dropped himself. His body met the stonework with a sickening crash. He lay still – his now glassy eyes staring skyward.

A sudden movement down the line turned all eyes. A surviving Free State soldier had broken cover and was taking off on a mad , desperate run. Another fusillade of shots. The man staggered and tumbled, rolling of the track and down into a water filled ditch.

Sean approached, Mauser at the ready, but stayed his hand. It was over. The man lay face down in the water, his body bobbing like a cork - his life's blood now darkening the dank green water.

"Flynn's dead."

Flanaghan drew firmly on his cigarette and sighed. For once Sean thought he detected a rare glimpse of compassion. Flynn had been showing signs of an anger and an obvious recklessness. News had come through of his family in the Belfast pogroms. The youth had drawn in on himself.

Another distant whistle blast interrupted Sean's thoughts.

Then a shout from a lookout. "Another train! A bigger one this time!"

"Right everybody into the hills and moving," called Flanaghan.

What about the weapons – that big Vickers?" asked Sean.

"No point! Too heavy and would slow us down. Besides where'd we get the ammunition?

★ ★ ★

The Free State troops had debussed and were now moving amongst the wreckage and the dead. One group was ascending the hill side in pursuit of the Republican Irregulars (as the Anti Treaty forces had by now come to be known). A Sergeant scurried down the track halting and coming to attention before his officer. The officer was Eamonn Plunkett.

"All our men are dead sir. Everyman riddled. They left one of their own. It's that Belfast lad Flynn sir. Why you remember him. He was with you in Dublin in the Rising."

"Flynn. Why of course. How could I forget him. Was wounded then. Survived only to die here."
Eamonn stifled an instinctive feeling of pity. He knew his Sergeant would not understand.
"Sergeant. Take a squad of men and secure the site. It'll take days to reopen this line. I'll take the rest of the men in pursuit. They think we don't know these hills. We all used the same hideouts once. This may take days. This may take weeks. But we'll get them."

Summer 1923

The cell was dark and austere. Its sole piece of furnishing was the hard pallet which served as a bed. Sean woke and stared at the cell's only light source, the small barred window from which now shown the soft grey light of dawn. He blinked in the half light. His head ached and his back seemed so stiff he had at first thought he would not be able to move. He raised himself up on his elbows. Then slowly he managed to sit up, his elbows on his knees, the palms of his hands cupping his chin.

Now his mind began to fill with questions. What had happened to the others? Had Flanaghan managed to get away? What would they do to him? He had heard storied of field executions. Summary justice meted out in the fields and hedgerows. Men tied up and dynamite tied about them. Was all this true? And what could he expect, he who had been so ruthless himself?

Voices sounded down the corridor. A strange chill gripped him. His questions he now thought must soon be answered. Footsteps – voices – coming nearer. Down the corridor cold and clear. They were coming for him.

Keys rattled suddenly and sharply in the lock and the heavy door swung open. From the darkness of the cell Sean now discerned a tall figure, dramatically silhouetted in the bright light of the hall behind. The figure was clad in a Free State

Army uniform, his greatcoat draped about his shoulders giving him an imposing, authoritative air. A strangely familiar voice spoke to someone else in the corridor,

"Wait at the bottom of the hall."

"Yes sir."

More footsteps – fading. Then more doors banging. Silence.

The figure in the doorway now entered the cell and moved toward the window. As he did so, Sean rose to his feet. The newcomer removed his cap and turned to face Sean. In the grey light Sean now recognized his old friend, Eamonn Plunkett.

"Hello Sean."

"Eamonn."

"'Tis sad that we meet like this – as enemies."

"What do you want Eamonn? Why have you come here?"

"But why not? My soldiers captured you. You're my prisoner. On the other hand we are old friends are we not? Why so suspicious Sean? Guilty conscience?"

There was a mocking ring to Eamonn's voice. Sean did not know if he should feel threatened.

"And just what have you in mind for me then?"

"Well I've been ordered to shoot you. You and that motley crew of yours."

The two men eyed each other warily. Eamonn leaned forward against the windowsill and put his head in his hands. Then he continued almost wearily, "The new Government is determined to rule. Its going to assert its authority – however painful that might be when one thinks of old friends. Sean, you and diehards like you must learn that it's finished."

"So to learn we must be murdered?"

"Oh for God's sake Sean, spare me that. You've been ruthless enough yourselves. You needn't moralise to me. This must stop. Look the way Ireland is to be ruled for the next century at least, has been decided – by the fates – by God – forces greater than we know. We've done well. We haven't got everything but we've got something we can build on – that another generation can build on. The country's exhausted. Britain's terms have to be accepted. You and your wild men must accept that."

Both men were silent for a moment.

"If I'm to die why the speech. An apology won't make it any better."

"You're not going to die. Not if I can help it. Now look – I can't do anything about your friends. But if you do as I say you'll make it. We were friends once. In a way I like to think we still are. Well?"

Sean was staring hard at the floor as Eamonn spoke. His mind was awhirl. Then Eamonn demanded,

"Well Sean what's it to be?"

Eamonn paused, clearly relieved that Sean had not proved stubborn.

I've arranged for you to be taken across country for interrogation. As you travel East your transport will stop and you'll have the opportunity to run for it. You'll be fired at as you run but the shots'll go high and wide."

"The guards?"

"We live in the world of favours Sean. Do a favour receive another in return. These are MY men – very much – MY men."

"How'll you explain –"

"Never mind. Never mind. I'll worry about that. But Sean when you do run for it, don't stop running. Don't stop till you've run yourself right the hell out of Ireland. Now come on. Let's go."

Eamonn turned briskly and strode toward the door, beckoning Sean to follow. They joined two army privates and walked out into a courtyard at the rear. The dawn was cold. A light freezing rain was falling. Descending a flight of garden steps Sean stopped and observed a group of huddled figures being force marched by guards down a secluded laneway. An ominous feeling stirred within Sean. He shivered and drew his greatcoat closer about him. A sudden dig in the ribs forced Sean further down the steps. One of the guards believed in using his rifle butt at least. Favours or not – they were still to be rough handlers.

As they approached an arched gateway two more soldiers emerged from a paved courtyard beyond. Both wore open greatcoats and their peak caps were pulled low over their faces. One had a Vickers machine-gun slung carelessly over one shoulder and dangled a cigarette from the corner of his mouth. His companion followed closely carrying an ammunition box. A machine gun belt was draped about his neck. Casually they saluted and passed by in silence. When they had gone Eamonn and Sean exchanged a nervous glance. They moved across the inner courtyard and through a large gate. Outside two Morrissey 'bull nose' trucks were parked by the roadside. A group of soldiers stood at the rear of the nearest one, idly chatting and smoking.

"Your transport," said Eamonn, "but first I think you ought to see something."

Eamonn ushered Sean to the far side of the trucks, away from the main group of soldiers. There on the ground, guarded by a single sentry, was a body. It was covered by a soaking canvas tarpaulin. On the ground the rain had washed blood over the courtyard tiles.

"Sentry! called Eamonn, and he beckoned for the canvas to be pulled off. Sean froze in disbelief. There before him, rigid, cold and gaunt was the body of Myles Flanaghan. Death had accentuated Flanaghan's skull like features, the skin pale and drawn, his wide staring eyes colder than ever. His tobacco stained teeth showed where his lips opened in that familiar, sinister smile. He had gunshot wounds to his chest. Sean also noticed one large wound behind his right ear.

"My men brought him in just an hour ago. Now Sean, believe me – it is finished," said Eamonn, moving closer to Sean, whose gaze remained transfixed on the dead Flanaghan. Even in death Flanaghan inspired a sense of awe, perhaps even of terror.

A sudden staccato of machine gun fire shattered the silence. Agonised screams briefly pierced the air. Sean turned sharply to face the courtyard where he had last seen his comrades. Death was working overtime that morning. Sean turned and seized Eamonn by the lapels of his greatcoat. His knuckles bared white and his arms shook as he and Eamonn glared at each other in a seething, silent rage. The sentry moved quickly to intervene but backed off as Eamonn held up his hand in a restraining gesture. Then Sean's stare suddenly softened and he released his grasp.

"Sentry." Said Eamonn, "put the prisoner on board."

Eamonn then moved away and after speaking briefly with

a corporal strode away quickly and entered the house by a side door. He did not look back. Sean climbed on board and sat on the middle of the buckboard. Two sentries sat at the back. The canvas flaps were drawn back so as to see out. The bullnose's engine started up and the little convoy moved off. As it jolted its way out into the lane Sean caught a glimpse of Eamonn, a solitary figure at one of the house's big French windows.

April 1924

he North Atlantic air was damp and chilly, the calm
sea a turquoise green. No horizon was visible yet.
A thick sea fog tapered skywards into a pale blue sky.
Sean had been up early and watched the sun rise from the
ship's stern. He stayed, staring after the ship's wake – the
following seabirds an encouraging sign of impending landfall.
He moved towards the bow of the ship. He passed a few other
hardy souls braving the morning chill. Now he looked
forward toward the mist, full of expectancy and a just little
trepidation. Soon through the mist the world's most famous
skyline would appear. Then he thought 'Miss Liberty and then
Ellis Island.'

He made his way back to the cabin. Andreena stirred from
under the sheets.

"Up so early?"

"Yes and why not?" said Sean. "The New World beckons."

"Let's hope we're welcome."

"We'll be fine."

"I was thinking of your dad's folks. It's one thing saying
yes from across the ocean, quite another matter when you land
at someone's door."

"We'll be fine. I'll not be overstaying any welcomes. I
should get work soon enough. Then a place of our own. We'll
be fine."

After breakfast Sean and Andreena found themselves on deck. More passengers now waited by the rails. The sea swell had gone and the ship's pace had slowed. The all pervading vibration of the engines had dropped.

"Well Sean! We got here. No U-boats – no icebergs."

"Darling I'm not sure that's funny."

"Wasn't meant to be. But just think of all the dying and suffering that there's been – out on that Ocean. Back in Ireland. In France."

"Well it's over now. Eamonn was right about that. Enough is enough."

"But Sean, will the rest of the world see it like that?"

"Don't think so darling. The Irish have no monopoly on madness, no matter what the poets say."

The ship's engine shuddered to bring about another drop in speed.

Douamont,
12 November 1924

The cemetery was swathed in a bright , luminous mist. The mid day sun was shining through the white canopy of low cloud. The mist seemed a strange companion to the rows of white crosses – endless rows disappearing into the mist. To Robert McBride the mist seemed a guardian, a massive burial shroud, protecting and somehow comforting the dead.

Some weeks earlier he had visited the British cemeteries near the Somme. Fallen friends remembered. This was another pilgrimage. This was his wife's lonely, despairing quest. She knew her brothers lay amongst the fallen. Their graves unmarked – all she could do was walk amongst the rows of the white, silent sentinels that marked the resting places of so many.

Robert had been distracted by a robin. The bird busily hopped or bobbed from cross to cross. The scene filled Robert with a strange sense of the eternity of things and a sense of renewal. His wife's approach ended the muse. Jeanette was dressed in black and so beautifully elegant in that. The beautiful brown eyes were filled with sadness yet her magic smile still shone through. They linked arms and turned towards the waiting charabanc. Then a short pause and another gaze at the silent scene.

"Pourquoi?" Jeanette whispered.

"Je ne sais pas."

"C'est fini?"

"Non. Malheureusement."

Brayspont – December 1924.